Man of My Dreams

Jenny Rabe

Jenny Rabe

This is a work of fiction. Similarities to real people, places, or events are entirely coincidental.

Cover design by Victorine Lieske. © 2018

To all the dreamers out there, who chase after what they shouldn't and end up with more than they think.

Chapter 1

Where are you, Rory?
It doesn't take a genius to get a signature.
Get it or else don't plan on coming back.

I read the three texts and then threw the phone into my purse. It was the fourth message from my boss, each one more threatening than the last. It didn't feel like much of a break to spend my lunch hour in the ER.

Millie had tasked me with the assignment of going to the hospital, getting a few signatures from a skier who'd had an accident on the mountain, and returning as soon as possible. Even though none of that fell under my job description, no one said no to Millie Perez.

As I drummed my fingers against the wall, I recounted the number of people in front of me. I was third in a long line stretching around the corner and winding around a potted plant. Each person waiting in front of me had taken precious minutes of the hour Millie assigned for this task.

"Ridiculous," I muttered.

The middle-aged woman in front of me turned and nodded. She looked as tired as I felt. Our silent disapproval of having to wait in a hospital line united us.

The automatic doors whooshed open, and the crisp, winter air rushed in to give me a break from the smell of sterile air and disposable gloves. The wind tousled my long, blonde hair around my face. After a glance at one of the office windows across from the line, I pulled it up into a tight ponytail. Millie demanded we look our best around guests at the resort.

I glanced at my watch again. It read 12:45. Millie was going to kill me if I didn't hurry and get back to—well, I wasn't sure what she wanted me to return to. Maybe more to-do items on her agenda? Definitely nothing that fell into my job description. *I'm an Event Coordinator, not a personal assistant.*

Another person moved out of line. I sighed. Two more people.

I tapped my foot along with the elevator music playing in the ER waiting room. *I just need to be clear with Millie about my long-term goals. She needs to know I'm in this job for the long haul. If she's trying to smoke me out, it's not going to work. I have history at the resort that she doesn't know about.*

When an ER technician in blue scrubs motioned me to move forward a few minutes later, I got a good look at her face. Though her spiky, short gray hair suggested she was a spry lady in her prime, her eyes were drawn down, and she rubbed at her temples. It wouldn't help to start on the wrong foot.

I plastered a smile on my face. "Hi, my name is Rory Lee. I need to visit Joe Murphy. He had an accident where I work, up at Ski Ridge, and I need him to sign some forms." I looked down at the legal forms Millie had pushed into my hands. I looked down at the legal forms Millie had pushed into my hands. I wasn't sure how I was going to get the guy to sign them, but she wouldn't take no for an answer, and neither would I.

The corners of the lady's mouth turned down, and I felt a wall coming up. "I'm sorry," she said in a flat, weary voice. "Our hospital policy states that you can't go into a patient's room unless you're next-of-kin."

"Totally understand," I said, knowing I couldn't give up that easily. "I'll be happy to stay in the waiting room if you'll just make sure he gets the forms." I felt embarrassed just suggesting the idea.

She looked up at the ceiling, then back at me. "That won't work either. For confidentiality purposes, I can't even verify if such a person is here. Try to contact him at home."

"Uh..." I couldn't give up now. I was so close. "Please. I am in kind of a pickle with my boss, and she never accepts no for an answer. Can't you help at all?"

She sighed and leaned over to whisper. "I know Joe personally, so I know he won't mind me telling you he is here. You could maybe wait in the lobby for him while I try to see if he's okay with you coming back, but it might be awhile."

There was not enough time to wait. And he wouldn't know who I was at all. No, that wouldn't work. "Thank you for trying," I said with a smile. "Don't worry about it." It wasn't this lady's fault that Millie expected the impossible.

Before I could say anything else, she lifted a hand to gesture the next person in line to step forward. The woman's face was full of regret. At least she had tried to help.

Time to try something different. Calling around for his number would be a nightmare, and I was sure Millie would be the key to finding it. That wouldn't work either.

I looked around the waiting room. There must be other ways to reach him. The waiting room was crowded, packed even. Every so often a door would open and a nurse would call back a patient.

Maybe it was time to wave the white flag and hope for the best. I checked my watch again, heat rising up my neck. Hadn't the ski resort hired a legal team to take care of potential lawsuits, or had Millie cut them from the budget too? But, oh, I really needed this job.

I walked around, looking for another way in. A Hispanic lady wearing a gray shirt with large white buttons and collar on the shirt and black pants pushed what looked like a wheelbarrow on four wheels into the emergency room. An idea came to my mind. I followed behind her, and when she looked my way, I lifted my resort badge, covering the front so she couldn't see.

"Admitting. Just checking on a patient," I said.

Last year, I had learned all about admitting girls

after being sent to the ER for a kidney stone and being sideswiped by one. Signing insurance papers while I was in major pain made her my worst enemy.

"Sí, yes, okay." The housekeeper moved to the side, and I passed, walking far enough away from her that I could breathe and think. I was in, but what did I do next? There were small rooms in front of me, some separated with curtains while others were individual rooms with two beds. Patients, doctors, and staff were everywhere. Panic flooded through me.

A tall man in a white jacket and scrubs breezed past me toward another doctor. "I'm here for Joe. Is he okay?"

My head snapped in his direction. The doctor showed him something on an iPad screen, they exchanged notes, and then the man started moving down the hall. I couldn't let him get away. He was my ticket inside. Without thinking, I scurried after him. *What am I doing? This is so* illegal. I crossed my fingers, hoping my impromptu plan would work.

The doctor's shoulders were wide, giving him a look of confidence even from the back. My heart raced as I rushed after him. The doctor had opened a door leading to a private room when I called out to him.

"Hi. Thanks for opening the door. My arms are full of these—"

The guy spun around, and I threw the papers past him toward the other side of the door. Legal mumbo-jumbo littered the floor around our feet. "Oh my gosh. I'm so clumsy." I rushed to the other side of the door to pick up the papers. He bent down to pick them up, and my eyes flitted from his tan shoes up to his navy blue scrubs and even further to his chiseled chin and flushed cheeks. *Whoa, holy hotness.*

"I didn't even know you were behind me. Are you okay?" he asked. His blue eyes were soft as he showed genuine concern.

Something about his face seemed familiar. Where had I seen him before? I glanced up at his name tag. *Dr. Camden. General Surgeon.* The name didn't ring a bell.

I shook my head as I gathered the rest of the pile and stood up. "Yes, I'm fine. Thanks."

He held out the rest of the stack with a wide smile that showed a little dimple in his left cheek. Totally swoon-worthy. His fingers brushed against mine, and a small chill crawled up my arm.

"Are you sure?" he said. "You look a little pale."

I was shaking all right, but it had nothing to do with dropping my papers. I nodded and looked past him into the room. No distractions. "Joe Murphy. Are you Joe?" I blurted his name out, hoping he could help me before the doctor could stop me.

The doctor's eyebrows jumped in surprise, and he let the door go. His light-blond hair made his blue eyes even more striking. "You're here to see Joe?"

I shifted my purse to the other shoulder. "Yes. I don't really know him, but my boss is going to kill me if I don't get his signature."

He stopped moving and spun around, blocking the patient in the bed from my view. Dr. Camden's pleasant expression was replaced with a stern look. "What?"

Oh boy. I never lied, and definitely never to a hot doctor, but it was either that or return to Millie empty-handed. "There was an incident at the resort. It shouldn't have happened because I told my boss months ago they should've taken care of it, but does she listen to me? No. And where does it get her . . . " I trailed off, realizing that I was starting to ramble.

"Hey, I think I've seen you around the resort," the man in the bed said.

Both of us turned toward the bed. I recognized Joe right away from the way his dark hair swooped wildly across his face. He had a muscular frame, built more like a body-builder than a ski instructor. He was one of the more popular substitutes, though I hadn't seen him at the resort this season since some of the courses had changed. Still, he should have studied the paths before taking a group down the mountain.

Whenever I'd seen him around the resort, he always wore a wide grin. Today, his face looked grim and pale.

Dr. Camden's eyebrows knit together, and his voice remained steady and low as he turned from Joe to me. "Joe, the other doctor said you slammed into a tree. What happened?"

"I haven't been to this resort for a while, and they changed their paths up. It was my fault for not checking the map."

"So then, the resort was negligent for not sending updated maps."

I swallowed hard. How had things gone sour so quickly? "He's an independent contractor. This is just—"

"This is just the resort covering its butt, making sure they're not liable." Dr. Camden's eyes shifted from the papers, then back to me. His blue eyes turned steely. "Right. Well, you can talk to him all you want, but Joe won't be signing anything."

"Oh, lay off her," Joe said. "Bring the papers over here, and I'll look at them."

A nurse was typing something into the computer on one side of the room, and Dr. Camden walked over to speak to her.

"I'm taking over for Dr. Martin, doing Joe's final assessment before discharge." His gaze never left mine for too long even as he talked to the nurse.

I ignored him and brought the papers to Joe. To my relief, he took them easily, sitting up straighter to read through them, then winced as his IV arm shifted. A large bandage stretched across his pale forehead.

"I'm Rory Lee, by the way. Sorry to hear about your accident."

"Thank you," he said, tracing circles around his IV line as he read.

I looked around as Joe read, trying to block out the doctor's glare across the room. The hospital room was small, with curtains to separate him and the adjoining patient, but the second bed was empty and the curtain pushed aside. The mint-green walls gave the room a sickly feel, but the windows helped brighten it some.

"Looks pretty explanatory," Joe said. "It was my fault. I should've been watching where I was going."

Dr. Camden crossed his arms. "You shouldn't be apologizing to her or anyone." His eyes continued to flit back and forth between me and the nurse.

"Am I good to go soon?" Joe said, putting the papers in order.

The nurse nodded. "Your skin is a little pale, but your blood pressure is holding and the pain meds are just setting in. You should be improving soon."

"Great," he said, smiling broadly. "Give me a pen, and we'll get you out of here too."

I handed him the pen I'd held tightly in one fist. My heart lifted. This was almost over, and then I could finally put this day behind me.

"Don't sign that, Joe," Dr. Camden said, walking over to the bed. "It's ridiculous that they'd follow you to the hospital. In fact, this has gone on too long. I'm calling security."

My breath hitched. Security? I hadn't planned on being thrown out of a hospital today.

Joe tried to stand and almost tipped over. Dr. Camden ran to his aid, helping him back into bed.

"What are you thinking, man? You just got seventeen stitches across your forehead. Lie down." He snatched the pen from Joe's hand before he could sign anything. I sighed under my breath.

"Oh, they're small stitches, Cam. Even you know that's not very serious. Now, leave her alone. Please. She's just doing her job."

And I was, though none of this fell under my job description as Event Coordinator. But lately, Millie had turned me into her private assistant, and saying no to her wasn't an option. I needed this job.

Dr. Camden grunted and turned his attention to Joe. "Your head CT scan cleared, so no concussion, but let me just check those stitches." He took a seat on the side of Joe's bed and checked the stitches crossing his forehead, blocking my view. "The resort is not at fault unless it was their mistake, right? You said it yourself, Rory. Your boss didn't follow through. That's not Joe's fault."

9

I bit my lip. Why had I told him that? He was no longer cute. Just super right and super annoying. Nervous energy bubbled in my stomach.

Joe gestured for Dr. Camden to move. "It's not her fault. I was aware of the policy. I signed the contract. Now, leave Rory alone. You're going to scare away the sweet thing. Look at her. She's almost in tears."

I rolled my shoulders back, knowing I had taken a defensive stance. I couldn't really be mad at the doctor. It was kind of sweet that he was going to bat for his friend. I just really hated being on the other side of this argument.

Dr. Camden turned, and what might have been a flash of compassion in his eyes left as quickly as it came. "Sorry. This isn't personal. You seem nice, but Joe's my friend." He dug out his cellphone. "Joe, which resort were you substituting at? I'll call my lawyer to take care of this."

"Ski Ridge."

Dr. Camden turned and fixed his eyes on me. "You work with Millie Perez?"

I nodded slowly. The doctor's frown deepened, and he seemed to be thinking hard. Did this sweeten the deal somehow? Or make it worse? Probably worse, if he knew Millie at all.

"Sign the papers, Joe," he said. He handed him back the pen and gave me a scornful look. "I want nothing to do with her, and neither should you."

Chapter 2

I crossed my arms tightly across my chest. The temperature in the room seemed to drop a few degrees as he spoke with a new edge in his voice.

"What did I ever do to you?" I said, my voice cracking.

"It's not you," Joe said, raising his IV arm and cutting me off. The doctor gave him a warning look, but Joe continued. "Cam, she needs to know it's not her fault."

"Anyone who gets into an accident at Ski Ridge is immediately sent here," Dr. Camden said, a little softer. "Let's just say I've had to deal with her too much lately."

Me too. I made an attempt at warming up to the doctor. "Yeah, she's not the easiest person to deal with." I bit my tongue. I had no reason to trust this guy. He could turn around and repeat everything to Millie. If she ever found out I was talking about her behind her back, my job would be toast.

Joe scribbled fast, going from page to page, and I appreciated his urgency.

Dr. Camden's pager went off several times. He read the messages, but continued to stay where he was. "Um, I'm sorry for being so . . . defensive.

His voice sounded less edgy, so I gave him a smile. "I get it."

"Why didn't Millie send a messenger to do her work for her? Usually she sends the legal team."

I tried not to bristle at being called a messenger. "She's been getting rid of staff to cut down on resort costs, so I wouldn't be surprised if she thought a legal team was unnecessary too."

Cam lifted his eyebrows but didn't say anymore.

When Joe handed me the signed papers, I checked the clock on the wall. I was well over the time Millie had given me. "Joe, it was nice to finally meet you, though I'm sorry it wasn't under better conditions. I appreciate your cooperation."

"See, you frightened her away," Joe said, chuckling at Cam. Then Joe looked at me with a gentle smile. "Rory, he's really nice. He's just going through a rough patch."

Cam clenched his jaw. "I don't see how that's any of her business."

Joe shrugged. "She needs to know that you're one of the nice guys."

Cam met my eyes. Despite his clenched jaw, I saw kindness. All he'd been doing was protecting his friend and trying to avoid a bad situation with Millie. I needed to take a page from his book.

My phone buzzed in my purse, reminding me of the consequences of ignoring Millie. "Sorry, I need to go. Dr. Camden, I hope things get better for you."

"Thanks." Cam's eyes softened, and he gave me his first real smile, showing perfectly straight teeth.

Our eyes connected, and my knees began to buckle. Holy smolder! I leaned against the wall to keep from falling. If he hadn't put up so many walls, I would've been putty in his hands.

His voice was gentle as he spoke. "Sorry for being a jerk."

"Um, no problem. I get it." I was almost out of there. Taking a few steps back, I waved goodbye. "It was nice to meet you both."

Before passing through the door, someone bumped me from behind, pushing me back into the room. I spun around as a woman with curly hair that fell to her waist rushed by.

"There you guys are! I've been looking everywhere," she said.

She reached back and caught my arm. Immediately, I recognized her brown eyes and dark complexion. My mouth went dry as I stared into one of the prettiest faces from high school.

"Rory, is that you?" Jasmine said.

Jasmine Guerro was everyone's favorite person back then and probably still was now. She was eccentric and fun, and talked so fast that it was amusing just to listen to her. And she remembered me!

"Wow, how are you?" I asked. "What are the odds of seeing you here?"

She hugged me close. Her floral perfume smelled strong and wild, just like her. I didn't remember her ever hugging me before. She held onto my shoulders and met my eyes "I know, right? I see old friends in the strangest places. Rory, you look fantastic."

I blushed. When had she ever given me this much attention?

"It's been too long," she said. "Don't you miss those high-school days?"

I held back a wry smile. She *missed* high school? "Yeah, I guess. So, what are you doing here? Are you friends with Joe?"

She walked over and planted a kiss on Joe's cheek. "Yep. This reckless goofball is my husband. Sorry I'm late. The line was ridiculous."

I covered my mouth, trying to hide my surprise. "Congratulations." Jasmine had dated more guys than I knew and didn't seem like the settling-down type. She smiled as I took this new information in.

"I know what you're thinking," she said, her smile growing. "But I am tamer these days. Joe and I married after our first year in college. How do you know him?"

Joe grinned and reached for her.

I shifted my weight. "We met today, though I've seen him a couple of times at the resort." I held up the signed papers. "Just picking up some waiver forms from him."

"Ahh, I see." She turned to Joe. "I think I've told you about Rory before. She was in my Spanish class in high school."

I nodded, a little surprised she would remember.

"Well, hang on a minute," Jasmine said to me. "Let

me deal with this real quick, and then we can talk."

She turned on Joe and started talking so fast I didn't have time to tell her that I had to leave right away. "You two better tell me what shenanigans you've been up to today. Something about hitting a tree? And why is my husband's forehead stitched together like some ragdoll's face?" Resting her hands on her hips, she looked from Cam back to Joe.

"Oh, the doctor did a better job than that," Joe insisted.

"Yeah, it doesn't look like a ragdoll job to me," Cam said.

They continued stuttering out excuses, but she cut them off with a wave of her hand. "I don't know what I expected when I got the call that you had been in a ski accident." She looked Joe over, fussing over the IV on his arm, the stitches on his head, even parts of him where there was nothing wrong.

Joe reached for her hands, stopping her inspection. She only half resisted. "Jasmine, baby," he kissed the front of her hand, "don't freak out. I should have studied the new course they built before taking up a group. I was out on the hill guiding a ski tour, and a tree reached out and hugged me."

I laughed, and Jasmine whipped around.

I closed my mouth. Had I just laughed out loud? *Shoot!* "Sorry. I was just imagining a tree hugging him."

Jasmine smiled, and I remembered how friendly she was. "It's okay. Just my luck that I marry a real adventurous guy." Her smile disappeared as she turned her attention to Cam. "If he hit a tree, then obviously he wasn't sent any notice of the trails changing."

Cam threw up his hands and sighed. "I said the same thing until I found out which resort he was at. Apparently, he was subbing at Ski Ridge today."

Confusion crossed Jasmine's face, then understanding. "I see. Well you and Millie never should—"

A voice called over the intercom, blocking out the rest of Jasmine's statement.

"Dr. Fisher, you're needed in the ICU. Dr. Fisher to the ICU."

The interruption reminded me I was still in the wrong place. "I better get going. If I don't return with these papers soon . . . "

Rustling the papers, I waved and headed for the door. Before I could cross the threshold, Jasmine called to me, "Uh, Rory, just a minute."

I froze, staring at the open door. Why couldn't I just make it out? Millie was really going to kill me.

When I looked back, Jasmine was sitting on the side of Joe's bed, holding both of his hands.

"We're taking Cam out for dinner since he's taken care of Joe, but I don't want this to be another third wheel date. I'm pretty much invisible when they're together. Will you come, and we can catch up?"

"Yeah, you should come," Cam said, his cheeks full of color once again. "I know I haven't given you the best first impression, but don't let that stop you. It's not your fault you work with Millie."

I imagined eating dinner across from him and dropping food down the front of my shirt or even worse, getting food stuck in my teeth. No, this was not a good idea. "That seems so fun, but—"

16

"Come on. Let's have a redo. I'm sure I didn't give you the best first impression."

A redo? That might be interesting. Obviously he wasn't a bad guy if Jasmine liked having him around. I looked to her, and she beamed hopefully at me. How could I say no to that? It would be great to have new people to hang out with. All I knew these days was work and home.

Joe gave me a weary smile. "Just say yes, Rory. Jasmine doesn't go away until you do what she wants."

She wagged her finger at him and then reached for his hand again.

It *would* be nice to have a change in my schedule. And it would be nice to see Jasmine again. And to give Cam another chance. "Okay, sure. Where should I meet you?"

I gave her my number, and she sent me a text with the address to the restaurant. "Six thirty okay?"

I nodded. "Yep. See you then."

After saying goodbye, I headed back to my car. A message from Millie buzzed on my phone, reminding me of my responsibilities. I opened it and read.

If you're not here in the next ten minutes, start updating your resume.

Chapter 3

I prayed no cops were on the road as I flew through the canyon. Would Millie really fire me? The ten-minute trip down Box Canyon Drive went quickly as I rehearsed my apologies out loud. At least the papers were signed.

Turning down the heat in my car, I cracked the window to let the cool breeze in. Mount Shasta, California was known for its low temperatures in the winter, but the start of this winter had been unseasonably warm. Our little city faced the mountain, the source of our main industry: outdoor recreation, specifically skiing. It was a hidden gem that only the best skiers knew about, though numbers were down this year due to weather and cutbacks.

Once I parked in my spot, I sprinted inside. Usually, I took my time walking to Millie's office, admiring the resort's fancy decorations or the koi pond where I liked to sit and think. Today, I ignored them completely. Trying to make it to the office as fast as I could, I ran past the guests hanging around the main entry hall where plush couches covered the floor and warm drinks were served.

"I hope those papers are signed," Mrs. Jessie said, giving me a sympathetic look. She'd recently dyed her roots blond, but her face was youthful and almost wrinkle-free.

She and her husband, Mr. Jessie, had run the reception desk as long as I could remember. Millie had cleaned house when she'd come a year ago, and they were the only two members remaining from the original staff that I had known years ago. Mr. Jessie had mostly gray hair, with a few streaks of black. He wasn't as young looking as his wife, being more stern and serious, but he always had a smile for me.

"I can't believe she sent you to the hospital to track down some guy." Mr. Jessie clucked his tongue and shook his head. "The things she makes you do, Rory. It makes my blood boil. If your parents were still here..."

"I know, but what else can we do? I don't want to leave."

The Jessies mumbled in agreement.

"There you are," another female voice called to me from down the hall. Brittney Felicie was my partner in crime and probably one of the most beautiful girls who worked at the resort. Her long, slender legs took fast strides towards me. I eyed her pantsuit with envy. Only she could've pulled that off. Not only did she look like a model on some runway, she had flawless skin and beautiful hair. Mostly she wore it in unique

African braids, but today she chose a wig with sleek caramel-colored hair that brought out the brown flecks in her green eyes.

"Yep, I'm back." I chuckled, seeing the desperation in her eyes. "Couldn't handle Millie all by yourself?"

She sighed, picking at her lips. She usually wore wild lipstick colors, but today she had forgotten to apply any. "No, that woman's out to get me. I have no idea how you put up with her. I'm tired of her calling me every five minutes."

Brittney was technically the person assigned to run *my* errands, but most days we were both more like glorified assistants to Millie and tag-teamed the brunt of the work.

"Millie's been asking for you for the last thirty minutes. I hope you have those papers."

I smiled and gave them all two thumbs up. "Yep, and I better get going."

They sighed in relief as I passed. While I sprinted up the stairs to her office, I glanced at my Fitbit watch counting each step. I'd bought it for myself last Christmas to help me prepare for a marathon, but work life had been too demanding. The distraction of watching my steps didn't help much, but the running gave me an extra reason to be sweating, other than facing Millie.

When I reached her office, Millie sat behind her desk. Her long, dark tresses touched the edge of the stacks of papers in front of her.

Breathing heavily, I took a seat in one of the two rigid chairs that faced her desk. I was sure she kept them extra stiff just in case someone thought they could get comfortable in her office. In contrast, her plump, leather chair towered above her glass desk, giving her an immediate air of authority.

"Sorry, I'm late," I said, forcing myself not to breathe too heavily. "There was… a lot of traffic." That hadn't been true. At this time of day, the canyon had been mostly deserted.

Cam's edginess paled in comparison to Millie's voice as she turned on me. "What competent assistant takes almost two hours to complete one task?" She paused, letting the insult settle before diving into the next one. "It doesn't take a genius to get someone to sign a piece of paper."

All thoughts of Cam flew from my head as fast as they'd come. Instead of defending myself, I let the silence resonate, knowing that's what Millie wanted. Any excuse I gave would have been a mark against me at this point.

Instead, I studied her face. Millie had greater fashion sense than anyone else I knew, which made it all the more mysterious why she hadn't learned the proper way to apply eye makeup. She had a soft, perfectly-round face, attractive at first glance, but when you met her eyes, every day was a new scary surprise. Today she wore smoky eyeshadow with overdrawn eyeliner. Thick, black lashes rimmed her dark eyes like hungry vines waiting to ensnare prey.

Thinking about her comical makeup gave me some relief from the serious situation I was in. No matter how verbally abusive Millie was, I needed this job. I wanted this job.

It was my dream to work at the same resort my parents had managed years before their car accident. The resort's name had been changed and the lounge

21

was more updated and chic now, but it still had a lot of the same qualities I remembered as a child. Plus, my mortgage was due in a few days, and this little city not only had limited jobs, but most of them were poorly paying jobs as well.

"I should fire you right now," Millie snapped. "Are you even paying attention to me?"

Too much attention. I pulled the papers out of my purse and held them out to her. They shook in my hand as she stared at them for a long minute.

Finally she took them, and I let my arm rest back on my lap. As she studied them, I stared past her at the view. It was no lie that Millie had the best view of the entire mountain. We'd only had two snowfalls so far this season and most of the trails needed extra from the snow machines. But ski season was in full force.

Millie snapped her fingers in front of my face, grabbing my attention again. "Head out of the clouds, Rory. Dr. Camden took care of the guy?"

I took a minute to shift in the chair to get feeling back in one of my legs. As quietly as I could, I tried to tap my left foot on the floor to force the tingling away. "Yep. There were no problems."

I studied Millie. Instead of her usual confidence, she appeared vulnerable and scared and her hungry vines were blinking faster than usual.

Millie released an exasperated sigh. "He didn't say anything to you?"

I shrugged. "What would he have said?"

She turned in her seat and stared out the window, lost in thought. "It doesn't matter," she muttered, more to herself than to me.

22

I stood up and nearly fell on my half-asleep foot. My eyes drifted toward the exit, only a few steps away. If only she'd tell me to go. I took a step toward the door. "Well, better get back to—"

Millie spun around and glared. "Yeah, you better. Let this be your warning, Rory. If you can't do a simple task, I don't need you."

I sighed with relief. "Thank you. I'll do better." My willingness to do her next bidding didn't improve the frown on her face.

She scowled at me before I could turn away. "You better. Check your desk for the next to-do list."

Without looking back, I saluted the air. "On it."

A soft, powdery snow started to fall on my way to the restaurant. It fell gently at first, small wisps of white powder barely touching the windshield before melting. But far too soon, those wisps turned into thick sheets, blinding my path.

As I rounded a curve, my car skidded to one side. I gripped the wheel with both hands and took my foot off the gas. My heart thumped as the skid stopped right before sliding off the edge of the road.

"Slow down, Rory," I said, chiding myself. Usually I was such a careful driver, but tonight I was late. Really late.

I shouldn't have been nervous, but I was. I'd never spent time with Jasmine outside of school, and now she wanted to go to dinner with me? What would we even talk about? I was sure she wouldn't know any of my friends, and we'd only ever been in a few classes together.

Cam's face flashed in my memory. We hadn't exactly started off on the right foot. Would tonight's meeting be just as disastrous?

Either way, I wouldn't find out if I didn't slow the heck down. I took my time driving the rest of the way and thanked my lucky stars when I slid into the parking lot.

I parked in the side lot with the two-dozen fancy cars already there. Mine looked like the only one from last decade. My eyes darted around the parking lot. Which one did Cam drive? Maybe the Mercedes or the Lexus? Or was he more of a truck guy? *Or maybe, he came with Joe and Jasmine, and I shouldn't worry about what kind of vehicle he drives.*

I climbed out of the car and pulled my thick bubble jacket closer to me. It wasn't the cutest, but it was the warmest. The air was too frigid in the canyon to care more about what people thought than for comfort.

Inside, groups of people waited to be seated, but Jasmine was nowhere to be found. The restaurant was decorated lavishly with hanging potted plants, tiny lights, and even a miniature waterfall at the edge of the waiting area. The leather benches that lined the restaurant were full with only standing room left in the corridor. Irritated people pressed against me as I scanned over the hungry crowd.

"Watch it," a harsh female voice snapped from beside me.

Turning to the right, I met the steely eyes of a lady dressed in mostly black. She had one of the sternest looks I'd seen since middle school, with her eyebrows scrunched together in a scowl and her lips pressed together in a tight line. She even had the stereotypical hook nose that some teachers prided themselves on.

I spoke, a little flustered under her haughty gaze. "Sorry, I didn't— It's really crow—"

She cut me off with a wave of her hand. Her stiff face seemed glued on. "Get out of the way."

My pulse sped, pumping hot blood through my veins as I watched her storm through the crowd. What a likable person. *Not!* If this was the type of people that hung out here, maybe I'd been wrong about coming.

I turned back to the door. What was I doing here? I barely even knew Jasmine. A hand touched my shoulder from behind, and I spun around to see Cam gazing down at me.

"Hey there, Rory." His warm hand sent waves of energy down my shoulder. His voice was friendly as he stepped closer so I could hear. "We're over here."

I stared up at my rescuer and gave him a hesitant smile. "Thanks. It's a madhouse in here."

He looked even more handsome than earlier, dressed in pressed khakis and a navy-blue, button-up shirt. His shirt sleeves were rolled to the elbow, and he wore a gold watch on one wrist. Expensive taste. The Lexus in the parking lot must be his.

His eyes sparkled as they met mine. "Glad you made it okay. It's really coming down out there."

I nodded, and he helped me out of my puffy jacket. "Thanks." I looked down at my jeans and red sweater. When I scored them at the thrift store a few weeks ago, I'd been proud of my finding skills. But now, I just felt underdressed.

He led me to our table, where Jasmine and Joe sat across from each other in a booth.

"Hey, you guys," I said, sliding in next to Jasmine. Joe was more casually dressed in jeans and a collared shirt, but Jasmine looked spectacular in a cashmere sweater and dress pants. Her hair was tied back with a clip, and she had gold, dangly earrings that fell past her ear. Yep, I was definitely underdressed.

Jasmine leaned over for a side hug. "I'm so glad you're here. Those jeans look amazing on you."

"I found them at Finders Keepers Thrift store. It's my favorite place to shop."

She beamed at me. "You're my kind of girl, Rory. I practically found my whole outfit there minus these earrings. These beauties were from Joe. He's got great taste, right?" She reached for his hand across the table.

Joe smiled and squeezed her hand gently. "For you? Anything."

"That sweater is a good find," I said, touching the fabric. "I can never find any worth buying, but this one is in good condition."

She nodded. "It was a lucky day. Rory, we should go shopping together sometime. I bet you'd be the best bargain partner."

My smile grew a little wider. She knew how to make someone feel like a million bucks with a few words. I eased back into the cushioned booth, no longer feeling self-conscious.

She kept on talking without realizing how much her words had boosted my confidence. "The guys have been talking about cars since we arrived. Please tell me you're not into cars."

I laughed. "Not a bit."

"We've talked about skiing too," Cam protested through laughter. He winked at me, or was it meant for Jasmine? Either way, I couldn't stop a blush from crawling up my neck. It was like I was meeting a whole new guy from the stern doctor of this morning.

I locked my eyes on Jasmine. Looking at her was safe. "Sorry I'm a little late. My cat hid my keys again."

Cam chuckled. "Your cat hides your keys?"

I sighed and grabbed a menu. "Almost every day. She's tricky like that."

"Where did she hide them this time?" Jasmine asked.

I frowned, remembering the dead spider I'd seen under the couch. "I'm not sure, but she eventually brought them to me. They weren't in her usual spots, so I feel like she's picking up her game."

Cam laughed again, and I found myself thinking of things I could say that he might find funny. Maybe he liked movie quotes? No, that was too cheesy. Or sport jokes? But I didn't know any.

Hold it. Just because a guy laughs at something you say doesn't mean they have a thing for you. An uncomfortable feeling settled in my stomach. This is what had happened last time, and the time before that.

The last time I thought I had a connection with a guy, I found him asking for the waitress's number on our date. Since then, I've avoided men and dived into work. It's more than enough to keep me busy.

A waitress came and took our orders. She brought us saucer-sized rolls that towered over my tiny plate. I buttered one, then took a careful bite, not wanting to spread it on my face as well. "Mmm," I said, moaning.

Jasmine looked over with a surprised smile. "Hungry?"

I nodded. "I skipped lunch today. And I was going to eat something before I came over so I didn't look like some ravenous wolf, but then Snowball . . . and the keys."

Cam pushed the basket of bread closer to me. "Eat up. There's plenty."

After the waitress took our drink orders, Cam started the conversation. "So, you and Jas were in the same Spanish class?"

With my mouth full of bread, I nodded to her to take the lead.

Joe reached for a roll in the basket and pointed it at Jasmine. "Wasn't she your partner for some presentation?"

Jasmine nodded. "Yes, and she saved our butts."

Biting my lip, I shrugged. Sometimes I annoyed myself with how straight of an arrow I was. Not a single B in my life. With Jasmine, I had pretended to need help so I wouldn't look like such a know-it-all. "She's pretty much the one who rescued the project. I was floundering at the time."

Cam smirked. "I think you're fooling everyone. You don't look like a girl who fails at anything. You weren't going to take no for an answer today at the hospital."

I paused mid-bite on my roll and gaped at him. *Am I that transparent?*

Jasmine shrugged. "He's right. You weren't failing.

You're the one who taught me all about those verb conjugations. I hated those. You always were modest, Rory, but it's okay to show off your skills."

My face turned beet-red. "Okay," I said drawing out the word, "time to turn the conversation to Joe."

The three of them snickered, but I was not keen to have any more attention.

"So where did you go to high school?" I said, shifting so I was facing him.

"I lived an hour south of here in the little town of McCloud. That's where I met Cam. He and I played on the same county baseball team. Now, we play on a city team together, but our season ended a few months ago."

Cam put down his roll and patted his stomach. "Speaking of, I have to make sure I keep running in the off-season or I'll be toast when it starts up again."

I checked out Cam's profile. He didn't look out-of-shape to me. "You run?"

"Yeah. I haven't done a marathon since moving here, but I like to run in the off season."

I glanced down at my Fitbit watch—anything to distract me from how handsome his face was. "I want to eventually run a 10K and maybe even a marathon, but I'm really struggling with motivation. I even bought this watch to count my steps, but that's about as far as I've gone." I held out my wrist to show him.

His eyes widened with interest. "Oh, yeah? I've got tons of advice if you want it."

The waitress came back with our drinks, and I ordered a steak and potato dinner when it came my turn to speak.

While Cam ordered, I thought about how

different he seemed now versus a few hours ago. His voice was kinder, and he was smiling. A gorgeous smile, in fact. Couldn't we just go back to him almost yelling at me? It was a lot easier to guess how someone felt about me when every word was said in frustration and anger. Between his eyes trained on me and the little grin on his face, I was second-guessing everything.

This is just running advice.

When the waitress left, Cam turned to me. "So you want to run a marathon eventually, right?"

I took a deep breath and nodded, preparing to give him my full attention. "Maybe one day." A second later, he motioned to Jasmine who scooted past me out of the booth. *Oh no, is he . . . ?*

When he plopped down beside me on the bench, I wasn't prepared for how nervous I'd be. The smell of almonds and cologne took me by surprise, and I couldn't help leaning toward him to get a better whiff.

"Do you have good running shoes?"

I tried to move my tongue, but it seemed glued to the top of my mouth. I'd look like an idiot trying to talk around that. I could only nod as he waited for a reply.

He grinned and shook his head. "You haven't even tried them out, have you?"

I shook my head and shrugged. It was true. They hadn't moved from the sneaker box since the day I bought them. And I had bought them at full price, which was a big deal.

Joe and Jasmine had started whispering to each other, glancing our way every few seconds.

Were they talking about us?

Cam didn't seem bothered by my nonverbal replies. Instead, he plowed on. "Well then, we start with breaking them in. You need to wear them. A lot. And not just for running. Wear them at work, around the house, and even better, on a run. It's like magic. The more you wear them, the more they encourage you to do more in them."

I thought of the heels I usually wore to work. Would Millie approve of me wearing anything that didn't make a sound when I walked? If Brittney could get away with her bold lipstick colors and wild outfits, why couldn't I wear tennis shoes?

Finally, my tongue fell into place and I could speak. "I could probably wear them on the days we don't have conferences."

He started into a list of things to do—something about eating healthy, interval training, and strength resistance—but all I could do was nod. I picked out the most important words he said, hoping he wouldn't ask any questions.

"Ready to make a schedule?" he asked.

Too late. The question sounded more painful than I'm sure he'd intended. I hadn't expected to commit to actually getting off the couch and doing anything, and here he was trying to write me out a schedule.

"Um, a schedule," I said, more as a statement than a question.

"You ordered the steak, sir," the waitress said, putting a plate in front of Joe. I sighed in relief for the interruption.

While she laid down our plates, Joe leaned over and whispered something across the table to Cam. I didn't hear everything, but I did hear my name and schedule, and I hoped Joe was telling him to simmer down. I wasn't ready for so much commitment. My job kept me busy, I doubted I'd have the gumption to follow a schedule even if I did have time, and I'd sure hate to let him down.

Joe must have said the right thing for Cam didn't bring running up again, and I was able to relax into the easy conversation that flowed as we ate. Cam and Joe joked about baseball, Jasmine and I swapped stories of thrift store finds, and we laughed as the boys argued about which teams had the best odds of winning the World Series the next year.

For dessert, we all decided to go in on the Bunker Hill's banana split. Twelve scoops of ice cream, six bananas, and twelve cherries, drizzled with caramel and chocolate dip, and covered in nuts. I took a few bites before I was full, but the two guys went at it like they hadn't just eaten steaks, potatoes, and full plates of vegetables.

In the middle of dessert, Cam's phone buzzed on the table. All talking stopped as we watched him. He looked at the front screen, annoyance crossing his face.

"Everything okay?" I asked as he continued to stare at the screen.

He nodded and slid it into his pocket. "Sorry about that. Gotta keep it on for work."

Joe brought up how Jasmine and he had met, and within seconds, we all shifted focus to them. Mostly.

"It was at the park," Joe started.

"No, it wasn't," Jasmine snapped. "You saw me at the movies, in line with another guy. And you walked right up to me and asked me for my number. In front of my date."

Joe smiled. "I love to rile her up. She gets so feisty."

The two began to bicker playfully, ending the argument with cute little nose kisses that made me yearn for someone to do that with me. I avoided Cam's eyes when I thought this, though I couldn't help but imagine doing those things with him.

When the waitress brought the check, I sighed. The food had been good, the company even better, and I didn't want the night to end. I'd even talk about training for a marathon again if it meant we could all stay and continue the conversation.

After helping me back into my jacket, Cam walked beside me as we followed Joe and Jasmine outside. The front entry was empty, and I thought of how earlier, all I'd wanted to do was turn around and go home. Good thing I hadn't. Tonight had turned out better than I could have hoped.

"So," I asked, searching for something to say, "why did you move here of all places?"

He shrugged. "It's pretty close to where I grew up. When I found out there was a fellowship opening at the hospital close by, I applied and got the job. It kind of just fell into place. Plus, it's got the best snow in around."

"Speaking of snow . . ." I trailed off as the four of us stared out at the blanket of snow that covered the cars.

"Wow, it really came down tonight. Drive safe everyone," Jasmine said, breaking the silence.

She gave me a hug, and I shook Joe's hand, knowing how awkward the gesture seemed. "See you,

Jasmine. Nice to meet you," I said.

"I'll call you next week and maybe we can go shopping. Then maybe after," she said using her index finger to point to the four of us, "we can do this again."

I brightened at the thought of hanging out again. "Yeah, absolutely. Talk to you next week."

Cam and I watched Joe and Jasmine cross the parking lot carefully, him escorting her with his arm.

"They're cute, huh?" I said, smiling.

He nodded, but his own smile wavered a little. "Where's your car?"

I froze. *Oh no, did he take that the wrong way?*

I pointed and started walking toward the back. "It's the old jeep over here."

He nodded. "I parked close to you. Let me get my scraper, and I'll help you clean off the car."

A second later, he whipped around and headed to one of the bigger trucks I had noticed earlier, two cars down from mine.

A truck guy. Tiny flutters erupted in my stomach as I watched him go to the back of his vehicle. I silently cursed as I opened the back of the car and grabbed my own ice scraper. *I do not like him just because of his vehicle.* I closed the door and started on one side of the windshield.

Cam joined me on the other side. "My uncle used to have a Jeep like this."

I cleared my throat, pushing down the knot that always formed when I thought about my parents. "It's an old one my parents gave me. A new engine later, it's still running."

"I'm impressed you've maintained it this whole time," he said, admiring it as he wiped it down.

A long stretch of an awkward silence fell, the only sounds being the scraping away at windows. It was peaceful and nerve-wracking at the same time. He looked over at me occasionally, a puzzled expression on his face. Was he waiting for *me* to say something?

"Anyway, welcome to Mount Shasta," I said lamely, picking up the conversation where it had died before. "I bet the hospital is glad to have you. You guys seemed busy today."

He nodded and gave me a guilty look. "Yeah, about today. Sorry for attacking you. I was just doing my job as best friend."

"I would've done the same thing." I put the scraper in the back and headed to my car door. Cam had already opened it for me. "Thanks, and thanks for helping me clean off the car."

He smiled. "You bet. Drive safe."

He started to close the car door, but stopped after a second.

"Did you . . . need something?" I asked after a few seconds of silence.

He ran a hand through his short hair. "I'm glad you came, Rory. When Jasmine invited you, I was a little worried that you'd think it was a date. I just got out of a bad relationship, and it wouldn't be a good idea to get involved again so soon."

My heart dropped like a rock in a well. A resounding thump still sounded in my ears as I tried to stutter out a response. *What did that mean?* "Oh, I didn't—"

I clamped my mouth shut, the indignation rising inside me. Who did he think he was? I hadn't flirted with him or given him any sign I was interested. So,

35

what was the big deal? "I honestly came because of Jasmine. Don't worry about me getting the wrong idea."

He sighed. "I'm sorry. That came out ruder than I'd hoped. I have a bad habit of encouraging women without meaning to, and I just wanted to make sure we're on the same page."

Now I was ready for the night to end. My cheeks burned. I must've done or said something to make him think I was interested. I grabbed the handle of the door, avoiding any contact with him.

"Thanks for your concern. You've been perfectly clear."

Chapter 4

I stopped by the ninnies' apartment on the way home. It was late, but I knew they'd still be up. I was too shaken up to be alone and needed noise. The three of them together would be enough to distract me until I was tired enough for sleep.

Dawn, Rose, and Mary were my mom's triplet friends from high school. Even though they weren't blood-relations, they took me in after my parents passed, and I would forever be grateful for their guidance and love.

I unlocked the door with my spare key. Their house was twice the size of mine and much more interesting. They had a wide entry hall with bright no-name artists' work hanging on every wall. A long hallway led to the front room where I knew they'd be sitting. As I turned the corner, I wasn't disappointed. They were in their usual spots.

The three sisters were the talk of the town, usually predicting events they thought would happen. It bothered some people, but I loved them.

"Hey, you three," I said, already cheered up by merely being with them. "Hope I'm not disturbing you." I settled at the end of the couch.

The three of them looked up from whatever hobby was resting in their laps.

Mary grunted, but I saw a smile tickle the sides of her mouth before she turned back to her medical journal. She was short and squat, with dark, short hair and thick eyebrows.

Rose, the tallest and kindest of the three, was painting the outside of a new flower pot, a contented smile resting on her lips. Her hair was tied in a simple braid down her back and not a single drop of paint was splattered anywhere close to her. "You never disturb us. It's been three days," Rose said, her musical voice singing in my ear. "How have you been?"

Before I could say anything, Dawn pushed Rose aside. "Oh, girls. Look in her eyes."

I stared at her wild, blonde hair sticking crazily out of all ends. Dawn was the enigma of the group, always surprising me with random facts or predicting the fortunes of someone in town. She set aside her fancy camera, a quizzical look in her brows.

Mary came up behind me on the couch, joining her sisters. I shrank under their stares.

"Ahh," Mary said. "Her eyes *are* different."

I leaned back on the couch and rolled my eyes. "What are you three ninnies going on about?"

"You met someone today, didn't you?" Dawn

asked, ignoring my question.

"Ahh, yes," the other two chimed.

I stretched out on the couch, putting my feet on the coffee table, the only worn-out thing in the house. I was used to their occasional fortune-telling, but it had been a while. When the ninnies continued to wait for an answer, I sighed. Maybe Mary had seen me at the hospital. She worked as an anesthesiologist. "Yes and no. But I'm sure Mary saw me and guessed that."

Mary straightened up. "You were at the hospital? Are you okay?"

I laughed. "You tell me. You seem to know more about my life than I do."

"Why don't you just tell us about your day?" Rose said sweetly.

"In detail," Mary said.

Rubbing at my temples, I decided to spill. It was better than them taking freaky-right guesses. I explained Joe's incident at the resort and the run-in I had with Cam.

"You met Dr. Camden?" Mary said. "Oh, I really like him. He's always calm during surgeries. And he's so handsome. And single, last I heard, though he's much too young for me."

I thought of the three separate interactions I had with him today. The protective, yet vicious friend, the nice but witty marathon runner, and then the man who rejected me before I even knew I was putting myself out there. I didn't know what to think about him. "He's okay."

I told them the rest of the story including the dinner and the parking lot scene. "I didn't think the night was anything more than friends getting together. But I must have been flirty if he thought it was something more."

The three of them exchanged looks, and Mary tilted her head to the side. "Maybe he's going through a rough time in his life."

I lifted my eyebrows. "His friend, Joe, said that he was, but he seemed perfectly fine at dinner. But then later, it's like a crazy switch flicked in him."

Mary shook her head. "I didn't say he was the smartest. This is just a guess, but you know how good of guessers we are, but I think he's worth the wait."

I doubted that, but I decided to drop the subject.

The next day turned out to be as troubling as the day before. Millie taped a to-do list to my door, more work for us on top of what Brittney and I needed to get done before upcoming groups arrived.

"Who made her upset this time?" Brittney asked, reviewing the list. Her iridescent purple lipstick glittered as she talked. She tried out a new wacky color every few days, and I had yet to hear Millie complain about it. If I came to work with orange or green lips, Millie would have something to say. It was probably because Brittney's lips looked better on any given day than Millie's scary eyes ever did.

Running a finger down the list, I read each item. "Nothing on here has anything to do with our events next week. Guess I'm not surprised. How about if you do all the office work, and I'll take all the hard-labor jobs?" I needed a chance to stretch my muscles.

She flicked her black braids to one side. "Girl,

don't overwork yourself. Hoping Millie will get a glimpse of you working so hard?"

I sighed. "Maybe one day all my extra hard work will pay off."

Brittney scoffed. "Yeah. I'll keep hoping for you. Now, you better get going, or we'll see Millie-zilla in no time."

I started my day by collecting drapes in the convention hall to be cleaned before our event next Wednesday. We had on average two groups who rented out the event space each week during the summer, having retreats or business meetings, and we were constantly in demand during winter since most businesses wanted to raise morale in the cold season.

I hated being on ladders, but it seemed Millie didn't feel it was part of housekeeping's job description to clean the drapes. Or maybe that was her justification for cutting more of the staff. I moved on to polishing the silver and counting the plates and silverware for the dining hall. Manual labor never bothered me. It gave me a reason to silently vent whatever frustration I had. And today I seemed to have a lot. Maybe I'd be an excellent marathon runner after all.

I was angry about last night, though I didn't understand why. The night had gone well enough but ended so wrong. His words of rejection plagued me as I continued to whittle away at my checklist.

Halfway through the day, I realized I needed the sign-up forms for the banquet next week. Unfortunately, they were locked in Millie's office. Most of my duties were done, and I couldn't wait any longer. At least all this walking would help me accomplish my Fitbit goal for the day—one thing Cam had suggested I increase. My stomach churned at the thought of him. Why couldn't I stop thinking about him?

I sighed and made my way to Millie's office. Her voice sounded all the way down the hall. But it wasn't me she was yelling at this time. I peeked into her office to see her on the phone. Her chair was turned away from me, but I could still hear everything.

"What do you mean?" she asked. "I thought we were going to try in a few months. Where did this come from?" It was quiet for a few seconds while Millie waited for an answer.

"Fine. Just fine," she said and slammed the phone down.

The door creaked as I leaned on it, and Millie whipped around with a mascara-streaked face. "What do you want?" Her voice sounded broken, more sad than angry.

Coming into the room, I dropped the list on a chair and grabbed for a tissue from a box on her desk. Sympathy welled up inside me, and I pushed it down deep. I didn't want to feel sorry for her. **But even if she was horrible**, she was obviously hurt.

"Are you okay?" I whispered, handing it to her. "Do you want me to get—"

"Just go," she said, ripping the tissue out of my hand, leaving me with a tiny scrap in my palm. She lifted her voice in a falsely confident way as she spoke. "I'll be fine. I always am." She wiped the tissue under her eyes, drawing a black smear across her face.

I shook my head, knowing she was lying. Even if

she wasn't the perfect boss, or even a good one, she was in pain. And by the looks of it, she had been in pain for a long time. "Well, call me if you need anything."

Who cared about the forms? I could get them any day. The nicest thing I could do was leave her in privacy. If she needed me, I had extended an olive branch. Without another word, I sprinted toward my office.

By the time it was lunch, my back ached and my only nice white shirt had dust smears all over it. I took my lunch onto the deck to eat. I loved watching the skiers come down the mountain, especially the more advanced skiers who seemed to dance across the snow.

I tried to picture my parents on top of the mountain, weaving in-between each other. The last memory I had of my parents was driving my Jeep to the resort during my junior year. We spent the evening skiing and ate dinner together as we reviewed and laughed at each other's falls and slips. They asked about school and boys, and we talked about vacation plans for the upcoming summer. I headed home after promises that they would be leaving work soon.

I would never forget the moment Officer Dan showed up at my door later that night. A storm had blown in that night, and on the way home, their car had slid off the ravine. The impact had killed them instantly. My life changed in so many drastic ways, and it was only now that I was picking up the broken pieces I had lost. Twelve years later, though it was still hard for me to think about them, it was also healing knowing I was working at a place they loved.

I looked away from the mountain and did a double-take. Cam was walking straight toward me. And he wore a subtle smile. I had to blink a few times to make sure my eyes weren't lying.

"What are you doing here?" Had he come to see me? No, that was crazy.

"Just checking on Joe, and I figured I would meet him here since he's still guiding on the ski trails. Anyway, I've been looking all over for you."

I lifted an eyebrow. *Why? I'm pretty sure you said what you needed to last night.* Now he was sending *me* mixed messages. "It's kind of soon for Joe to be hitting the trails again."

Cam shrugged. "The crazy guy insisted that stitches couldn't stop him. That man's a mess, but he never gives in."

I nodded. "He's dedicated, that's for sure."

He seemed to consider me for a moment. Then he said, "I'm actually a little surprised I've never seen you here before. Joe and I ski up here all the time."

"Well, I'm always here. Maybe it's because I stay inside most of the time."

He laughed. "And I try to avoid coming inside."

An awkward silence passed between us, yet he didn't leave. What did he want?

"Millie's never talked about me before?" he asked. "I thought you would have recognized me by now."

Why would Millie ever talk about him? She seemed to hate him as much as he hated her. "Um, nope. I don't, but I should probably get going." I gathered my things and stood, but when I tried to move away, he blocked my path.

44

He sighed. "I did it again, didn't I?"

I cocked my head to the side, confused. "Did what?" His face was full of remorse, like he had kicked a dog or something.

He sat down and tapped the chair I'd just been sitting in. "Will you sit? I need to tell you something."

I returned to my chair, though the seat didn't feel nearly as comfortable as it had before he'd walked in.

He wiped a hand across his face where chin stubble would have been. Today, his face was smooth and handsome. "Joe tells me all the time I have a very abrasive personality. I'm blunt and to the point, and most of the time, I am unaware of how it affects people. I hurt your feelings last night, and I didn't mean to."

Well, that was a surprise. I relaxed against the chair, a little more at ease. "Don't worry about it. Blunt is sometimes good." If nothing else, I knew exactly where he stood, and I knew there was no chance for us. It took the pressure off.

"Good day today?" he asked, changing the subject.

I remembered Millie's tear-stained face and frowned. Not really, but I wasn't going to tell him. "Yeah. I've been using some of the running tips you gave me last night. I've already doubled my step count for the day. I even broke out my shoes."

I moved my tennis shoes from under the table to show him.

"Alright, those are good shoes. And you were just letting them sit in a box?"

I smiled and hid my feet again. "Better late than never, right? I've already doubled my steps."

Cam sat back in his chair and seemed to be deep

in thought. Finally, he said, "You know, they have a great indoor track inside the hospital. I can get you a pass if you want." His eyes glistened in the light, looking like a moving ocean.

"Really? A full track inside the hospital? How can they afford that?"

Cam chuckled. "It's a preventative measure, I think. Just trying to extend lives and keep the staff strong. Plus, there's not much to do here in the winter time."

"Well, I was going to sign up for a gym membership," I lied. I was very opposed to paying someone else so that I would be able to run. It should be the other way around.

He crossed his arms over his chest. "Why? You can come to the hospital for free. Come on. Let me get this pass for you, especially since I've been so off-putting since the moment you met me."

My resolve melted at his apologetic tone and his offer of a free pass. It probably wouldn't hurt to work out in the same place he worked. The hospital was big enough that I probably wouldn't even see him. "Well, it *is* on my way home."

"I'll meet you down in the waiting room around 5:30. Sound okay?"

I nodded. "Sure."

He gave me one last, soft smile. "I hope Millie's not too rough on you today."

Speak of the devil. Millie walked out of the elevator at that moment and headed straight for me. I had to get out of here before she saw me and thought I was wasting time. I stood and started gathering my things again.

He stood as well. "Is lunch over?"

I nodded and tried to back away from the table, bumping chairs along the way. "See you later."

Millie stalked toward me, her heels clicking. "What are you still doing here?" she said. Her voice echoed throughout the room, and time seemed to stop. Eyes turned toward us as she continued to raise her voice. "Don't you have a lot of work to get back to?"

I winced and finally met her eyes. Wait a minute. She wasn't looking at me. All of her anger was focused toward Cam.

He checked his watch, seemingly unconcerned by her attack. "I was just leaving. Had to check out Joe's stitches before I returned to work. I heard the trail wasn't properly marked."

Millie laughed. "Yeah, well it's been a little busy around here . . . you know, running things on my own."

Cam snorted. "Like that's a problem. You love that you have the final decision."

I backed against the wall next to me, hoping I could melt right into it or become a fly on it. Millie's makeup had been redone, and her lashes were coated with a thick glop of mascara. The two of them had fire in their eyes I hadn't ever seen in either one of them, and hoped to never see again. What was their history together?

"The more you come around, the more I hate you. I don't want to see you on this property ever again. You can manage things from your end far away from here."

Cam cleared his throat. "I think that's for best." He

47

gave me a half glance before leaving, looking more apologetic than angry.

Millie huffed, then turned to watch him leave as he brushed past her.

I stood there, mentally twiddling my thumbs and concentrating on not breathing too heavily. How many sides to Cam were there? I was just about to back away when she swiveled around.

"Rory, what were you doing here?"

Caught. "Well, technically I was just eating here in the loung—"

"Did he say anything to you? About me?"

I swallowed hard. Anything I could say would not be good. Best to lie. "No, he just asked about the food."

She smirked. "What an idiot. Word of caution, don't talk to him again if he comes back. You're better off staying far away."

I nodded. She glared at me, her thick lashes making her eyes look like two dark pits in her face. "Isn't your lunch break over? I thought the drapes would keep you busy all day."

I pulled my leftovers tighter to my chest, as if they could protect me. "Better get going on that list." I scooted away before she could say anything else. There were serious issues between Cam and Millie. A deal gone bad? Had they been involved in a dating relationship? A business deal? My thoughts swirled around me like falling snow, all of them convincing me that going to the hospital and seeing Cam was a very bad idea.

Chapter 5

I had somehow kept Cam out of my thoughts since I left my office after lunch. That is, until now as I sat in the car debating whether I should meet Cam at the hospital or not.

Millie was a hard person to please, so I had to give Cam the benefit of the doubt. On the other hand, I knew I should stay away from him. He was confusing, and there was obvious conflict between him and Millie. I didn't want to be tangled in any relationship they might have had.

I started the car and headed home. Why rush things? I could wait another day to see how I felt. Plus a workout and sweating at the gym with strangers was about as tempting as working another twelve hour shift.

Since it was the start of the weekend, I decided to treat myself with Thai takeout. I ordered pineapple fried rice, pad thai noodles, and mango sticky rice for dessert. Once I was home, I fed Snowball and then collapsed in front of my couch in my PJs and turned on *The Bachelorette*. What could I possibly need that wasn't in front of me?

A few minutes into my show, my phone buzzed with an unfamiliar number. It was still early in the evening, but too late for an unknown number. I ignored it and continued to eat. However, I noticed that each of the three subsequent times the person called, they wouldn't leave a message. Stored in my phone was every one of Millie's numbers, so it couldn't be her. When it called for the fourth time, I finally answered it.

"Hello," I said, tentatively. When no one answered right away, I almost hung up. But then the person spoke.

"Is this Rory?" a familiar male voice asked. I dropped the pad thai box, spilling noodles all over the floor.

Cam?

"Crap. No, Snowball, get back. These are not for you." The cat scurried away, but hid around the corner where he could glare at me.

A chuckle sounded on the other end of the line. "Is your darn cat up to no good again?"

I straightened, dropping my rag. "Cam, is that you?"

"Hey, Rory. How'd you guess?"

"Your laugh," I said without thinking. Too many guys had annoying laughter that either sounded like the air was being squeezed out of them and they were wheezing to death or was a strong imitation of a dog's

50

bark, loud and annoying. Cam's chuckle seemed just right.

There was silence on the other end. "Is something wrong with it?"

I bit my tongue. Why was I giving him more reasons to think I was interested? "No, sorry. Never mind. How did you get my number?"

This time the sound was more of a nervous chuckle "Yeah, um, I asked Jasmine. I thought you'd be stopping by for the gym pass, and I wanted to make sure I didn't miss you."

Leaving the noodles on the floor for now, I perched at the end of the couch, antsy all of a sudden. "Staying at home eating Thai food in PJs sounded so much better than running. I'm sorry."

He cleared his throat. "Well, I'm sure I didn't make things easy today. Millie hates me and I'm sure she's warned you. I'm afraid I put her in a bad mood. You didn't deserve that."

The digesting noodles churned in my stomach. There he went again, showing a sweeter side. "Thanks. For saying that. But I've dealt with Millie for over a year. I'm practically an expert."

Cam laughed again. "Tough girl. I like it."

I moved the phone away and stared at it. Was he flirting with me?

Snowball came from around the corner, darting eyes at the abandoned noodles on the floor. I dropped back to my knees and started scooping them up with my free hand.

He cleared his throat. "I'm hoping we can start over, you know, a fresh slate. I think I spoke too soon the other night."

Spoke too soon? What is he talking about? I wasn't sure I wanted to know. I grabbed a dishrag and started to wipe up the rest of the mess as I waited for him to continue, but he didn't. Finally, I asked, "So did you need something?"

"I was wondering if I could bring that pass over? I'm leaving the hospital in a few minutes."

"Oh, you don't have to—"

"Please. Maybe if I bring this to you, we can talk for a minute and you can get to know the real me. Walls down and everything."

Warning bells rang in my head, and the reminder to stay away from Cam pounded in my head. "I don't know about that."

He sighed. "Look, I know what Millie must have said about me, but I promise I am a decent guy. I'm actually leaving town and just wanted to drop this pass off before I go. I feel I owe you a little explanation and a chance for you to see things from my side."

He was leaving town? I looked down at myself. Plaid PJ's and an old, Christmas T-shirt. At least it would send a very platonic message. "Um, I guess that would be okay." I gave him my address and waited as he typed it in.

"Whoa, I wish I lived that close to the hospital. Sometimes driving through the canyon every day is a pain."

I laughed. "I know the feeling. You know, you can just leave the pass at the hospital's front desk, and I'll pick it up." It wasn't too late to evade his invitation one more time.

"No, it's alright. I'll be heading that way for my trip anyway. Be there in about thirty minutes."

After saying goodbye, I surveyed the room. My mind whirled. How had this night gone from comfortable to daunting in sixty seconds? I stared at my step-counting watch, trying to focus on something other than my beating heart. Cam was coming here.

He was just dropping off a pass. He probably wouldn't even stay long. He did say he wanted to talk. I glanced around the room. I wasn't a neat-freak, but it looked clean enough. I'd need to run the mop over the floor and maybe brush my hair. And probably change. I wanted to still look casual, but in retrospect, my PJs were old and a little see-through. I didn't need another layer of awkward. Thirty minutes wouldn't be much time at all.

Half an hour later, I had slipped on a pair of jeans and a hoodie from college, cleaned the front room and kitchen, and turned the TV back on. I wanted to be doing something other than twiddling my thumbs when he showed up.

When the doorbell rang, I sprang to my feet and opened the door. He stood there, bundled up in a black overcoat and scarf. His cheeks were red and shiny.

"You look cold. Come in."

"Thanks." He stepped in and closed the door behind him. "Is this *your* house?"

I nodded and pulled at the strings on my sweatshirt as we stood there, staring at each other. Oh, this was not a good idea. "Yeah, I grew up in it."

He smiled. "It's cozy." Having him in my house made it seem so much smaller.

"So, you wanted to talk about something?" I started. The sooner this was out, the better.

53

"What has Millie told you about me?" he asked.

I shrugged. "Not much, actually. She asked if you had said anything about her at the hospital. You didn't really, so she dropped it when I had nothing to say. And then today after you left, she warned me to stay away from you."

He sighed in relief. "That's it?"

"Is there more I should know?" I asked. I couldn't keep the suspicion from leaking into my question.

He shook his head quickly. "Not really. The two of us had a business venture together that tanked, and now we're not speaking much."

I lifted my eyebrow. Was that the entire story? "What kind of business venture?"

"Just one of those projects in college where you have to work as a team. She kind of stabbed me in the back, and we just fell away from each other."

I sighed. If that's all it really was, that wasn't so bad. I bit my lip and looked toward the couches. Sitting would be much less intimidating than standing next to him. "Want to sit?" I asked.

That seemed to snap him out of his thoughts, and he backed up toward the door again. "I should probably start on my trip. I just wanted you to be able to use the pass while I was gone."

"Where are you going?" I asked, trying not to sound too interested.

He jiggled his keys. "Somewhere warmer for a few days. I need to get away and clear my head."

I nodded, though I didn't understand. "Well, I hope it's helpful."

He pulled out a card with my name etched on it. "Anyway, here's your pass."

"That's really nice. Thanks. Have a safe trip." I twiddled the card in my hands, the plastic cold in my fingers.

He backed away a few steps but didn't say goodbye. "Rory, I wanted to ask you something."

My eyebrows pulled together. "Sure, what's up?"

"I know that I said I wasn't interested in more than being friends, but now I know I was wrong. I want to give us a fighting chance."

My heart thumped loudly in my chest. Was he saying what I thought he was saying? My throat was dry as I asked a follow-up question. "A fighting chance? For what?"

He sighed. "I'm not very good with words. Jasmine is going to ask if you want to hang out on Thursday and go to that store you two like. Then I was hoping that afterward, we could all hang out together, maybe go skiing?"

My chest tightened. I hadn't skied since my parents died, not even once. "Um, I don't know. I'm not that—"

His eyes lifted in interest. "I can teach you. Or Joe can since he's an instructor." He paused and then said in a softer voice, "I really want to take you out. On a date," he added.

My heart leaped in my chest. I pushed that feeling down deep. This was not time to get excited. I had misunderstood before. "But the other night you said you weren't interested in being more than friends. And what about Millie. If she sees me with you, and you two have had some issues together, won't that be bad?"

"That's why I think I spoke too soon. Why not get

55

to know each other while I'm figuring all my crap out? I mean it's just one date, right?"

I shrugged. Dating wasn't exactly what I wanted right now, but it'd been so much fun to hang out with Jasmine and Joe the other night. There was still one very big reservation. "But Millie. She's my boss. I can't—"

He nodded. "She doesn't ski, and we can stay away from the inside of the resort just in case she's there. I would take you somewhere else, but this one always has the best snow."

He was right about that. But that didn't solve my problem with Millie. "And what if she sees us together?"

He crossed his arms and leaned back against the door. "She never works late any night, and rarely visits the ski slopes. We'll never see her, and if we do, what does it matter. We're just skiing, right?"

"How do you know so much about Millie's schedule?"

He looked down at his hands, not meeting my eyes anymore. "I've made it a point to know where not to go. Oil and water and all that."

It would be fun to pick up skiing again. And where could I feel closer to my parents then on the hill where they'd loved to ski?

"Will you help me learn the ropes?" I said with some hesitation. I still wasn't sold on this idea, but I had to admit it sounded fun. Especially if he was the one teaching me.

"Of course."

There was no really big reason to stay away from skiing. Mom and Dad had met on the hill, laughed on the hill, had loved that resort so much. They wouldn't want me to stay away from it. Why had it taken so long to even consider skiing again? What better place to feel close to them than on the hill where they met?

Cam waited patiently as I considered all of this, studying me with a half-smile on his face. He really was so handsome. And even if he was a little abrasive, when was the last time I'd had a little mystery in my life? It was time to start living.

"Alright. Let's do it."

Chapter 6

Time seemed to crawl at turtle speed after that night. Since Cam was away, I had every reason to go to the gym and try it out. After a day with Millie, I had enough stress to work out, but didn't want to go to the track alone. So I ended up at the ninnies' house most nights or calling it an early night and going to bed so that the next day could come and go.

Jasmine called on Tuesday, as Cam said she would, and we made plans to meet up before going night-skiing with the boys. Jasmine didn't say much, but I could tell she was excited Cam was taking me out. I don't know what I was more worried about—skiing for the first time in ten years or skiing with Cam.

Cam sent me texts throughout the week now that he had my number. Each time I received one, I felt a little thrill reading his words.

During the day, they were short and barely went beyond small talk.

Have a great day.

I never felt like I could do more than send lame, stilted replies. *Thanks. You too.*

But at night, our texts became longer and kept me thinking long into the night. Mostly about what our favorites were. Favorite spot to go when we were upset. Favorite song to listen to when we were happy. Favorite place to eat at when we were starving.

I learned he loved the lookout at Piedmont Hill, the one that showed a broad picture of the city. He also liked rock music when he was feeling good and burgers when he was starving. They were small things, but each piece gave me greater insight into him.

Since Thursday promised to be the absolute worst day of work, I relied on re-reading his texts from Wednesday night to get me through the day.

When I walked in that morning, Ms. Jessie's face confirmed what I already knew. Millie's temper had been bubbling all week.

"She's on one today, honey," she mumbled to me when I walked past. "You watch yourself."

I nodded and sped up, skipping the elevator to take the stairs instead. I checked in our office for Brittney before I remembered that she had taken the day off for her birthday. Was that the reason Millie was upset? I did most of the grunt work anyway, so I didn't see why Brittney's absence would be a problem.

I sat down to check my email, only to get a text

from Millie.

Meeting in my office. Now!

Well, that was fast. I logged off my computer, grabbed my stylus to take notes with, and boogied down to her office. She was tapping her nails across the desk, lost in thought, when I arrived. She didn't look up when I entered.

"I'm here. What's up?" I asked, a little disheveled from the run. I sat down in the chair and met her eyes, then gasped. For the first time since I had met her, there was not a single trace of makeup on her face, leaving her looking very vulnerable. Finally, after a tense moment, she spoke.

"When two people make a contract with each other, a promise together, they are committing to working it out, even in the rough times. So, tell me, Rory, since you're so smart and seem to know everything about anything, why do people try to ruin something that is working just fine?"

I shrugged, having no idea what she was talking about. "Maybe the person didn't know what they were getting into?" Maybe that's why her project with Cam hadn't gone well in college?

She huffed. "Oh, he knew. That's why this is so infuriating. And then they cover it up with secrets. I mean, do they think people won't eventually find out what they're doing?" She glared at me across the desk, her lips pressing into a tight line.

I swallowed down a lump growing in my throat. I hadn't really promised her I wouldn't see Cam, but surely she couldn't be talking about that. I didn't even know how I felt about him.

"Is someone keeping secrets from you?" I said,

trying to keep my voice stable and confident.

Millie sighed and laid her forehead on her desk. "Yes, you idiot. Why do you think I'm so upset? He's lied about everything." She pounded her fist against the desk a few times.

Relief washed over me and then understanding. This must be about her fiancé. "Is everything okay? With you and Phillip?" I added lamely.

As if I had flipped a switch, she started crying, hiding her face in her arms.

After a few seconds of doing nothing, I came closer to her desk and dared to pat her on the shoulder. "It'll be okay."

Almost immediately, Millie froze under my lightweight touch, no longer making a peep. Her dark hair covered her face, and she seemed to be steadying her breathing. Was she actually listening to me? Would this finally be the moment we bonded?

I reached for a tissue and laid it on the desk near one of her fisted hands. "It's okay. Everyone goes through issues in their relationships."

Her eyes peeked at me from between thick strands of hair. "Issues?" she said, her voice scratchy and tired. "Who said this had anything to do with Phillip? What are you doing here still?"

"I . . . you—" This woman was impossible to please. I hadn't brought up her drama, she had. I just happened to catch her at a vulnerable time, and now she was blaming me?

She stood up suddenly, pushing away my arm as if it were a fly. The tissue flew off the front of the desk. She stood tall, despite her tear-streaked face. "Phillip and I are absolutely perfect. I shouldn't have said anything to you. This is a personal matter."

Then why did *you bring it up? Just let me do my job.* I pushed the indignation down and tried to keep an even tone. "Well, what did you want then? You texted me to come in here."

Her chest rose and fell a few times before she looked at me with a glare in her eye. "I've changed my mind. I'll email you the responsibilities delegated to Brittney instead. You can pick up her slack for today since she is out." She swiped hard at her face without batting an eye.

I knew I should try again, just to make sure she was really okay. "Are you sure you're—"

"Of course I'm fine," she snapped, cutting me off. "If something was wrong would I be here, doing my job? Now, get going on your own responsibilities."

I turned away from her without another word, convinced I had done my best to be supportive. It was only after I turned the corner from her office that I heard her crying again.

When my end-of-the-day alarm went off at 4:45, I sent Millie an email of what I had accomplished today. Not everything was checked off, but I had made a dent. We had new clients set up to visit the resort in a month, and the Ruschter Bank team-building event for next week was finalized and ready. Now it just needed her stamp of approval.

After shutting down my computer and gathering my things, I made a beeline for her office. If I hurried, I'd still be able to meet Jasmine at 5:15.

The lounge was busy as I passed, most skiers either warming up after a long day or gearing up to go outside. Soon I would be with them, though I would avoid the lounge completely. If Millie was still here, it probably meant she was going to stay for a while, no matter what Cam had said about her leaving early on Thursday nights. But my worries were unwarranted, and her office was dark and locked when I showed up a minute later. I breathed a sigh of relief and headed to my car.

Now for the fun part of the day. The Finders Keepers thrift store was in the old part of town, hidden between the old movie theater and a clothing store for older women. It was my favorite part of town, and its rustic look matched the winter setting. Small flakes of snow started to fall as I parked my car outside the thrift shop. I looked up the weather and inhaled quickly at the forecast. A blizzard was scheduled to hit around nine tonight. Hopefully, we would all be home before it really got bad.

Jasmine was waiting for me inside the little shop, already browsing through a rack of extra-discounted items. She turned to me with a plaid shirt on a hanger. "Too retro?" she said, a little smile tickling the corners of her mouth.

It was one of those picks that a grandma would have worn in her later years. I gave her a wry smile. "Did Joe age thirty years overnight and you're trying to impress him?"

She giggled and put the shirt back on the rack. "Yeah. Maybe in a few years I could make it work."

Although I was a little apprehensive about hanging out with just Jasmine, I shouldn't have worried. We fell into an easy conversation, laughing and talking as we searched the racks.

"So what are you looking for today?"

Jasmine shrugged. "I don't know. I thought I'd just browse."

I gasped in mock horror. "You should never do that!"

"What?" she said, almost laughing. "Why?"

"These three friends of mine taught me the right way to shop at a thrift store."

Jasmine lifted her eyes in interest. "The right way, huh?"

"Browsing is okay, but I try never to go into a thrift store without something I need in mind or I end up buying too much or not getting as good of a deal. Today, I came with the purpose of getting a snowsuit for skiing tonight. Mine's a little tight."

"Oh," she said, looking toward the ceiling. "Well I guess I do want a bigger frying pan. Joe is always making these amazing skillet dinners, and he complains he never has a big enough frying pan."

I nodded. "Let's find it then."

"Okay, but let's look for your jumper first, just in case we run out of time. Joe made me promise that we'd meet him at 7:00."

Luckily, there was a rack full of snowsuits, most of them for younger kids, but there were a handful of adult sizes, and I chose two jumpers to try on. The navy blue one fit perfectly, and even had a half-off tag.

We weren't so lucky finding a pan but we made plans the next week to search again since every week brought something new. On the way out, she caught me by the arm.

64

"Do you live near here?" she asked.

I nodded. "Yeah, a few minutes that way." I pointed south. "In an old neighborhood by the tracks."

"Why don't I follow you home, and Cam can drop you off later tonight? That way we don't all drive there."

I nodded. This would solve my problem of Millie recognizing my car if she happened to show up, though I wasn't sure she knew what my car looked like. "Yeah, that sounds good."

"Then it will feel more like a date," she added, a smile creeping onto her face.

I blushed as that realization settled in. After a week of texting Cam, I was eager to see him in person.

Chapter 7

I dropped off my things inside and invited Jasmine to wait in the front room while I changed. I quickly dressed in my new snow pants and added a pair of lime green gloves and a matching hat that my dad had given me for my sixteenth birthday. Just wearing them made me feel closer to him. Why had I waited so long to get back to doing this?

I grabbed my other gear, hoping it wasn't a dead giveaway that I was a little experienced. It would be fun to have Cam teach me and would distract me from thinking of my parents too much.

After feeding Snowball, we hurried out to Jasmine's car.

"Whoa, it's really coming down," Jasmine said. She lifted her hand to the sky. "At least skiing in the falling snow is a blast."

I eased into her car after she unlocked it, not feeling as confident about the weather as she was. I just hoped it wouldn't hit us hard and block us in the canyon on the drive home. The roads would be slippery and dangerous, especially at night. Now it would be extra hard to keep my parents far from my thoughts.

"So what kind of music do you like?" Jasmine asked, flipping through her channels.

When she got to one that had a familiar song, I said, "This one is great. I love soft rock after a long day."

She started the car, revving it a little more than usual. Then she sped out to the main highway.

I rechecked that I was buckled and held on to the door handle for good measure.

"Hard day, huh?" she asked. "Millie must not be nice to you either."

I let go of the door handle after she stopped at a traffic light, then ran a hand through my loose hair before wrapping it in a tight ponytail. The extra time gave me a moment to consider how to respond. "It may just be that I'm her employee. She keeps everyone at a distance."

Jasmine grunted but didn't say anything more.

Finally I asked, "How do you know Millie?" Maybe she'd give me a clue as to why Cam and Millie disliked each other so much.

She cleared her throat as we continued to wait. "Well, I guess I don't know her that well anymore. She's changed a lot since we first met. Cam, Joe, Millie, and I used to hang out, more so in college than here. Cam made a business deal with Mille that turned out badly, and ever since then, we haven't really met up.

I nodded. "He told me something about it the

other night. Do you know what kind of a deal it was?"

She lifted an eyebrow. "I bet he'll tell you if you ask him, but it's not really my place to tell you."

The light turned green, and she sped off down 12th street. The street eventually led to the mouth of the canyon where the plows hadn't gone yet. The road was packed with snow, and I could only hope they weren't icy yet. Her car was 4-wheel drive, but the first time it skidded, I grabbed the door handle again.

"Are you okay?" she asked, her eyes flitting from my hand to the road again.

Swallowing down the tight feeling in my throat and ignoring the pang in my chest, I decided to tell her the truth. "When I was in high school, my parents got in a car accident on this road. I've tried to get over my fear of driving in snow, especially since I work in the canyon, but it's hard to fight your past."

"Oh, I do remember hearing about that." Jasmine swerved to miss a car that had crossed too far into our lane. She eased her foot on the brakes, but we still skidded for half a second. "Sorry," she added.

I took deep breaths and looked down at my fingernails. Everything was fine. Everything was going to be fine.

She slowed down significantly after that, taking extra care around the corners.

"So you knew about my parents?" I asked, glad for a distraction. I was the quiet girl most kids didn't remember after a school year ended. My group of friends and I had been close, but they had escaped town as soon as college hit.

She gave me a small smile. "I know we weren't close in high school, but your mom was one of my little brother's teachers. He always said how much he loved Mrs. Lee."

I smiled too, remembering my mother as a teacher. She loved teaching 5th grade, and she was good at it too. It didn't surprise me that she was well liked. "My dad used to manage Ski Ridge. My mom would come at nights and help out, and I worked there almost every summer. I guess I came back to feel closer to them."

Jasmine's eyes seemed to mist as those words sank into the quiet. After a minute, she said, "No wonder you are willing to put up with Millie. Well, I hope it works out for you. I'm almost positive Millie will get bored with this venture, and then you can take over as manager."

Oh, how I wish that could happen. Though I was completely interested in one day becoming a general manager, I knew I needed more experience. Millie had made some good changes to the resort, minus letting go most of the old staff. Our events were consistent and not only paid for themselves, but gave the resort a nice cushion.

"Anyway, please don't tell Cam about my parents. I guess I'll tell him if we ever get to that part."

She smiled but kept her eyes on the road. "I hope you do."

We made it out of the canyon not too long after that. I started to wring my hands together. It had been a few days since seeing Cam, and even though I was excited, I knew things with him could go either way. We could have a great time and hit it off well, or this could be another misunderstanding and I could read everything wrong . . . or he could.

69

Chapter 8

We parked in the visitor's lot among a sea of other cars. The magical experience of skiing fresh snow at night was simply too popular for most people to sit out.

Jasmine got a text just as we parked and read it before we got out. "Joe said they're waiting for us at the ticket counter."

My stomach did a flip-flop. He was here? Already? If I was this nervous, maybe I wouldn't have to fake being a beginner.

I grabbed my gear, as awkward as it was, and tailed Jasmine all the way to the ticket booth. We dropped our gear just as Joe called out to us.

"Hey, girls," Joe said, kissing Jasmine first, then reaching over to give me a side hug.

It was hard not to like Joe. I stepped back and then saw Cam peeking out from behind Joe. He looked even cuter than I remembered. He wore a black snowsuit and gray jacket, but his eyes were what drew me in. Blue eyes that were captivating, vibrant, and electric.

"You're back," I said, my voice a little shakier than I would have liked. His smile widened, sending an influx of butterflies to my stomach.

"Hey there." He took a tentative step forward, holding out his arms for a hug. Instead of feeling awkward, I seemed to fit perfectly. He held me tightly for a second then released me but his scent of laundry soap and mint lingered with me as he backed away. "Just got back a few hours ago. Glad to be back."

We stood there studying each other for a second.

"That green looks great on you," he said, gesturing to my hat and gloves. He held up his own gloves and hat. They were forest green but his goggles were rimmed in lime green. "I guess we can skip the favorite color talk."

Heat crawled up my back and neck, as his gaze never wavered. "I guess we have that in common."

He smiled and gestured to the counter. "Tickets are on me today, guys. And by the looks of it, you don't need any rental equipment. Are you sure this is your first time skiing?"

I froze. This was the part where I talked about my parents, but no words came out. I wasn't ready for this.

"Well she does work at a ski resort, and we picked up a few things at the thrift store," Jasmine said, coming to my rescue.

He eyed my feet with interest as we began to make our way up the hill to the bunny slope. "Those

71

are Black Diamond boots. I haven't seen that brand in a while."

Glancing down, I checked my boots. I hadn't worn them in almost a decade, and though they were a little snug, they still fit. They had been my mom's when she was younger. I didn't know what brand they were until now, but Mom had mentioned plenty of times that boot companies didn't make boots that well anymore.

"Well, it was a thrift store. Maybe someone was cleaning out their closet," Jasmine said, saving me again.

Finding my voice, I lifted my skis. "I guess I got lucky."

Joe clapped his hands together. "Well, let's go. The slopes are calling me."

We reached the top of the bunny hill, where we dropped our skis and poles. People milled everywhere, even with the darkening sky and continuously falling snow. The ski lift was busy, and the trails were full of what looked like tiny black ants tumbling down the hill. This close to the familiar atmosphere of the ski hill, with snow falling gently, it was magical.

I felt Cam come up behind me, bringing even more heat to my face as I realized how close he was. If I fell back, even a little, we would touch. Just to experiment, I stepped back and bumped right into his chest. Instead of moving back, he held onto my waist and held me against him. He was warm and soft, and I didn't want to move away. I folded my arms across my chest to hold in the heat.

"You're cold," he said, his voice making me jump.

And then his arms were rubbing mine. My heartbeat rattled inside me. I took a deep breath. *He is just warming me up. It doesn't mean anything else. Chill out.*

I hesitantly relaxed against him, leaning into his chest. His smell, his touch, everything about him made my head spin. If the rest of the night went this way, there was no way I could talk myself out of dating him. I was a goner.

"Uh, well, looks like you two are good up here by yourselves," Joe said, interrupting our moment.

We whipped our heads around to where Joe and Jasmine stood next to us, skis already strapped on and goofy grins on their face. Cam dropped his hands, and I took the time to put on my gloves and hat.

"We're going up the hill for a bit while you help her learn the ropes," Jasmine said, her smile as wide as ever.

Cam nodded. "Are you still up for learning to ski?" he asked as they skied away.

I laughed. "Sure, though I'm not sure I could ever beat Joe."

We watched the two of them race down the bunny slope toward the lift at the bottom of the hill. Joe was fast and efficient as an instructor, but he slowed his pace to hold Jasmine's hand and lead her down the bunny hill. It was a small slope with three small hills, and a few cones were scattered at different places for the beginning skiers.

"Where should we begin?" he mused aloud.

"Um, well, I've sat through a couple of the sessions, you know, because I work here. I've learned how to do the pizza when I stop, and I've watched a lot of skiers fall, so I know not to do that."

He laughed, filling the silent night with his voice. I knew that skiers were all around us talking and laughing and the ski lift creaked as it moved, but all I could hear at the moment was him. I shivered with excitement.

"Well, maybe let's start by going down the hill. If it gets too rough, just go into your pizza formation."

I nodded and picked up my ski poles. Then a little clumsily, I slipped my boot into the first ski. It snapped into place just fine, but as I turned to step into the next ski, I fell forward.

Cam moved quickly, grabbing me close to his chest again. I looked up at him just as he smiled down at me. "Trying to get into my arms, huh?"

I giggled. "No, just slipped."

"Right," he teased, holding on to me for a second longer. Then he held out his hand and said, "Can I help you?"

I looked down at his gloved hand. "Thanks." I stood up with his help, but moved forward on my own, leaving him behind. It only took a few seconds for him to catch up. Despite my experience, I was rusty and clumsy. I didn't fall, but my pizza move needed some work.

"Wow, you're a quick learner." He caught my waist right before I toppled over, and I gratefully held on to his hand after that. There was no need to get hurt when he was just being helpful. At least that's how I justified holding his bulkily gloved hand in mine.

At the end of the bunny hill, there was a ramp treadmill that moved you back to the top. I climbed onto the ramp first, and he stepped behind me, standing close behind me.

The treadmill shifted, sending me sprawling backward into his chest. He laughed and helped me back to my feet. "Steady, there," he said, his voice tickling my ears.

When we made it to the top, he led me to the other side of the ramp where there were no practice cones and the hills were a little bigger. "Should we try?" he said, gesturing to the hill. "You did so well over there, I think you can handle it."

I shrugged. "Let's go."

His eyes lit up with interest. "A real adventurer, huh?"

I gave him a sly smile and fled down the hill away from him, skiing faster every second. The wind blew in my face, my feet plowing through the snow on my way down. It felt fantastic. I heard the whoosh of skis behind me, but I didn't stop until I reached the bottom of the hill.

I stopped in perfect formation and spun around. Cam was staring wide-eyed at me.

"You've skied before haven't you?"

When I met his eyes, I knew I couldn't lie anymore. I didn't have to tell him my whole life history. Just enough. "It has been a while, but yes, I know how to ski. A little."

His jaw clenched. I shifted my weight a few times before he spoke again. "Well why have we been wasting our time on this dinky hill?" he said, smirking. "Time to go up the mountain."

He sped off toward the lift, and I followed him with my eyes but didn't move. Going down the small

75

hill was one thing, but going on the ski path? I wasn't ready to make a fool out of myself. After a few seconds, I trailed behind, though a little reluctantly. Had I already screwed things up?

He waited for me at the bottom of the hill, and then, silently, we moved into line. Joe and Jasmine saw us and skied back to be behind us.

"How was it, guys?" Jasmine asked.

Before I could answer, Cam's eyes lit up. "She's a natural, though, she's totally skied before."

"Sorry I lied," I said, lamely. I gripped my poles tightly as I waited for his reply.

He shrugged. "You could've just said it's been a while. I don't know why you felt like you had to."

Jasmine nudged him from behind. "And miss out on a private lesson with you? I would have done the same."

A small smile spread across his face. Even if it wasn't the whole truth, he seemed to like this fib a little better. "Well, I'm glad you lied then."

Jasmine leaned over to whisper in my ear. "You should have just told him."

I awkwardly turned to tell her that I didn't know him well enough when my skis started sliding out of line. Cam reached out to steady me, keeping hold of my waist until it was stable.

Our turn to step in front of the ski lift. He reached for my hand and helped me ski to the position where the lift scooped us up onto the bench. And then, suddenly, it came, and I fell backward. Cam held out a hand so I wouldn't fall forward since there were no bars across the front.

I wrapped an arm around my side of the pole and

held it tighter as the lift rose higher. Skiers got smaller as the lift began to climb. I looked down and immediately shut my eyes and held the pole tighter. This part had never been my favorite. I'd always imagined myself falling off a lift and breaking every bone in my body. My dad used to hold a hand out in front of me so I felt safe when I was younger. What I wouldn't have done to have him here with me now.

Cam chuckled. "Whoa, you really haven't skied in a while, have you?"

His voice was gentle again, and I risked a glance up at him, not releasing my grip on the side of the bench. He was watching me intently, his grin fading into concern. He scooted closer, and hesitantly wrapped an arm around my shoulder. "Hey, it's okay. I won't let you fall."

His tenderness was too much, and I had to look away.

I tried to relax, but my head was fuzzy. Something was bothering me, and it had nothing to do with the dozens of feet of empty space below us. The real reason I hadn't wanted to talk about skiing was because I doubted I could without talking about my parents also.

Before I could pinpoint how to fix the problem, the ski lift dropped us off. I was a little unsteady as I put my feet down and pushed off the little hill, but I was determined to do it alone.

The drop-off came fast, and I turned my feet in just the right way so I was able to push off and get out of the way before the next bench behind us hit me. I skied to the side and waited. I may not have wanted help getting off a lift but going down the mountain by myself was a death sentence waiting to happen.

Cam tried to catch my eye, but I was too nervous scoping out the downward death-drop in front of me.

"My dad and I used to go skiing all the time," he said.

I turned my head so I could hear him better, but kept my gaze on the hill in front of me.

"Now that he's gone, I always try to do the first run for him." His words came out in little puffs of smoke.

I looked at him then. "You do?"

He nodded. "It's my way of remembering him."

I smiled then, an idea forming in my head. This first run, and every first run after, would be a way of remembering my parents too. It was the perfect time to tell him about my parents.

But too soon, Joe and Jasmine whizzed up behind us, and the moment to share with him had passed.

"Are you ready, girl?" Jasmine said coming up behind me. She eyed me with concern, probably noticing the tears forming in my eyes.

"You don't have to do this if you don't want to," she said, quietly. "I will totally ride my butt down the hill with you if you want out."

I shook my head. "I'm going to do it. For them."

She looked at me a moment before smiling. "Okay, then. Cam, why don't we go down the left side? It looks less bumpy."

He nodded, agreeing. "Let's do it."

The four of us pushed off down the hill. My heart leapt in my chest the moment my skis started moving. It was like riding a bicycle after many years of staying away. Everything just came naturally. I followed behind Joe and Jasmine, with Cam behind me, but after a while, I forgot they were there.

The wind felt sharp against my face, with snow hitting me at every angle. It was amazing. The snow beneath us was fresh and smooth, and my skis seemed to fly down the mountain. We dodged around the lift poles, picking up speed as we descended. The end came way too fast and before I could stop myself, I slammed into a big pile of snow at the bottom of the hill, tumbling over it and laughing at the same time.

Cam slid down next to me, a worried expression on his face until he saw my smile. "Good stopping there, Rory."

I laughed again, and he helped me to my feet. "Want to go again?" he asked, his eyes brighter than ever.

And right at that moment, I knew this was more than just friends. I liked him. I really liked him.

"Please," I said. "A dozen times more."

When Joe and Jasmine suggested getting some food an hour later, I shook my head. We were on our seventh run before my legs started to give out. "I better not. My legs feel like jelly, and I have a big day tomorrow."

I could've sworn I saw Cam's lips pull down in disappointment, but maybe I could ask him to come inside for a while. We said a quick goodbye to Joe and Jasmine and headed off toward the truck. Before I could get in, Jasmine ran over to me and pulled me aside.

"Cam, she'll be right there," she said to him. "We just need to schedule our next shopping date."

Then she turned to me with that convincing look

in her eye, and I knew this would have nothing to do with a shopping date. Still I tried.

"So when do you want to go shopping—"

"You haven't told him yet, have you?" she said, cutting me off.

"Whoa, you don't beat around the bush, do you?"

Jasmine shook her head. "You two have amazing chemistry. Trust him." She reached for my hand and squeezed it, filling me with courage.

I nodded. "Okay, I'll think about it."

Chapter 9

I did think about it, for half a second. But then the weather got to me. The snow was falling fast, blinding Cam as he drove out of the parking lot. To his credit, he went slower than Jasmine, but still not slow enough. Entering the canyon sucked the bravery right out of me, and I clung to his truck door, not making a peep.

Thoughts of my parents' accident after a night of skiing with them ran through my mind like a freight train. What if the past repeated itself right now? My nerves were on edge every time he took a new corner. The truck slid every few seconds, and I gripped the edges of his truck tightly.

"Are you okay?" Cam said. "You haven't said a word since we got into the car."

I nodded, but didn't say anything. When he continued to try at a conversation, I gave him clipped answers, continuing to eye the side of the road. After a while, he stopped trying to make small talk, turning on the music to a low hum. By the time he put his truck in park outside of my house, I had finally decided it was worth the risk.

I relaxed against the seat and sighed, rubbing a kink that had started at the base of my neck. Cam didn't turn off his engine, but he looked my way. This was the time. I needed to tell him, I knew it now. Honesty was the start to any . . . friendship.

"Do you want to come in?" I asked.

He chuckled. "I'm surprised you want me around. You were so quiet on the ride home that I could've sworn you were going to jump out of the truck any minute." His voice sounded softer, hurt even.

I turned toward him and blurted the first thing that came to mind so he knew none of this was his fault. "My parents died in that canyon. I always have a hard time driving through it when it's snowing real bad."

"Oh, Rory." He rubbed at the scruff on his face and looked back out the window where the snow was coming down in waves. "We should go inside and talk, but I need to check in with the hospital. I just got a page from them a few minutes ago."

Disappointment spread through me. I'd just shown him a big part of my heart, and now, there was a good chance he'd leave and it would remain out there, raw and exposed.

"How about if I meet you inside in a minute or two and let you know?" he asked. "Either way, I'm going to change out of this snowsuit and finish listening to your story."

"Okay." I got out of the truck and almost fell when my legs thudded to the ground like wooden blocks.

He laughed and joined me on my side of the truck. "Ok fine. I'll walk you to the door and then change."

I half-giggled, half-grimaced as my legs jerked and stumbled down the stairs. They weren't used to feeling so tired. "Good training for a marathon, right?"

"Oh, that's right. Did you use the gym while I was gone?"

I shook my head, not wanting to lie again. "I didn't want to go alone."

His eyes twinkled down at me. "Well, we'll have to make sure that won't happen this coming week."

I pulled out my keys. Well, at least he wanted to see me again. The door unlocked quickly, and, within seconds, Cam had disappeared into the snow again.

Quickly, I slipped on a pair of jeans and an old sweatshirt from college. By the time I put some water on to boil, I heard him knocking on the door. I hurried to open it.

A gust of wind and flurries filtered in along with Cam. I shut the door behind him. "Whoa, it's really storming," I said, shivering.

"So, what did you want to talk about?" he asked, running a hand through his hair, making slush run down his face in a stream. I was tempted to wipe it away for him. "The hospital wants me on call. Every time there's bad weather, we're bound to have more patients."

My shoulders fell. "Oh, that's a bummer."

He shrugged. "I've got some time. The weather channel predicted sixteen inches in the mountains, so I will have to run home to get some things before they shut the canyon down. But let's not worry about that right now."

I nodded and looked around as he did, taking in the small rooms. Being a doctor, he probably lived in something much nicer. My shabby furniture and beat-up floors needed a facelift.

Snowball came into the room and started lapping at the tile floor where water dribbles from Cam's shoes had made small puddles.

He leaned over to pet her. "Hi, Snowball. Nice to see you, kitty." Snowball fell at his feet, allowing Cam to rub him.

I snickered. "Now, you're never going to get him off you. By the end of the night, you'll be covered in white fur."

"That's all right. I love cats."

Warmth spread through me as he smiled at me. He really wasn't so bad. Uncertain and a little guarded maybe, but surely not as terrible as Millie had said. Maybe I should stop listening to her voice inside my head and do my own thing for once.

The teapot whistled from the stove. "You can hang your jacket up there," I pointed to the rack on the door, "and I'll get some hot chocolate for the two of us."

He glanced down at me, his eyes piercing mine. His cheeks were red and flushed with the cold, and it made him look even more adorable.

"I'll meet you on the couch," I said.

I broke away from his intense stare, spinning around to go into the kitchen. I went through the motions of filling the mugs and adding a few marshmallows, all the while rehearsing in my head what I would say.

By the time I made it back to the front room with two mugs, he was mopping up the puddle on the entryway floor. Helpful *and* handsome.

"You didn't need to do that," I said.

Holding a mug to him, I switched it for the mop, which I then put back into the closet. After joining him on the couch, I set my cup on the coffee table and faced him. I needed a warm -up before I revealed everything. I grabbed a stack of cards on the side table, more to distract myself. It was an old set of Go Fish cards from my childhood.

He smiled when he saw me holding them. "You want to play?"

I grinned. "It might be easier to play a light-hearted game while we talk about this. I love Go Fish, and I happen to be very lucky."

"I'm sure I can take you," he challenged.

With a shrug, I dealt out the cards. For a few seconds, I relaxed and enjoyed a simple game with him. His knee pressed casually against mine, but neither one of us moved away. A step in the right direction.

"Do you have an octopus?" he asked.

I looked at my cards and smiled. "Go fish." I waited a few seconds for him to draw, then asked him for a dolphin. He handed me two with a wry smile on his face. As our fingers touched, a tingle crawled up my arm. Then I asked for a starfish and a dolphin. And the tingles didn't stop. There was something between us, and I was sick of denying it.

"How about a starfish?" I said, eager to touch his hands again.

85

"Finally," he mumbled, though his face twitched with a smile. "No starfish. Go fish."

Beating him with a few more plays, it was just enough time to gather my courage. After I laid down my last set and called the game, I cleared my throat. "Ok, I'm ready to talk now that this game has given me courage."

He chuckled. "Good, because I don't think I'd like losing cards to you again."

I laughed nervously. "I told you I'm always lucky."

He grabbed for his hot chocolate. "I guess so."

I stacked the cards and slipped them back into their case, all the while rehearsing how to start what I needed to say. I put the deck to the side and looked up at him.

"Today was a mile marker for me. It was the first time I've skied since my parents died." I paused as that soaked in. "That's why I didn't want to tell you I've skied before. I thought separating the now and then would make things easier."

He looked up from his drink, and, a second later, put it on the coffee table next to mine. "Rory, I'm sorry. I would've done the same thing." He held out his hand for me to take.

I took it, the warmth of his fingers crawling up my arm. It was soft and comforting all at the same time.

My voice sounded strangled as I continued. "We were really close, my parents and I. We went skiing together all the time. That equipment I have was my mom's when she was younger. When they died, I felt like I lost so many parts of me."

"So, you said they died in the canyon. What happened?" he asked.

86

"They were driving home from work during a bad snowstorm, and their truck slipped off the side of the road and into the ravine."

Recognition dawned on his face. Cam's gaze was softer now, and he pulled me into his arms. "No wonder you didn't want to talk in the truck."

My throat started to close up, but I swallowed the hard knot growing there and kept talking. "One of the reasons I put up with Millie as much as I do is because my parents used to manage Ski Ridge and being there helps me feel close to them."

"Wait, what? They used to own Ski Ridge?" he said, sitting up, forcing me to sit up as well.

I nodded. "And when they died, we found out how bad the resort was doing. My parents had put a lean against the house to pay the staff at the resort. It was during a bad recession and that's the way they paid their bills. When they died, we sold the house—and everything really—to rid their names of any debts. I only just recently bought it back."

I glanced around the room. I had almost gotten things back the way they were, but it was still so different. "It sounds insane when you think about it. I'm trying to get my old life back so I can feel some normalcy again."

He squeezed my hand. "You know that business venture I told you about, the one that failed with Millie?"

"Yeah," I said hesitantly. "The one in college."

He sighed and put his mug down. "Well, it's been a little more recent than that. The resort you work at, the one Millie manages, it's the business venture we went into together."

I sat there, stunned at this new information. "Wait, you own the resort then?"

"Not technically. I own shares of the resort, though when things started to go sour a few months ago, I've been working on selling my part, but Millie refuses to work with me now that things are over between us."

We sat there for a few minutes, sipping in companionable silence. I could have stayed right there all night. But after a while, my curiosity began to grow. If I was opening up, maybe he would too.

"Okay, can I ask you something now?" I said. He nodded, a pained expression crossing his face. "I didn't want to ruin any chances with you by bringing my baggage into this."

My mind spun in whirly circles as I tried to process this. "So you and Millie were together?"

He nodded, pinching his lips tightly together.

"And you're not now?"

He nodded again. "Our breakup was a long time coming, but once we were business partners, it added too much stress, and I really couldn't see any benefit to staying together." Cam blew out a heavy breath and dropped my hand so he could cover his face with both hands.

"Is that who texted you at the restaurant?"

Cam clasped his hands together in his lap. "You saw that?"

I nodded. "It was hard to miss the annoyance."

"She's having a harder time letting go, making sure she rubs my nose in this decision, but I don't regret it."

"But she's with someone else now. She's even

engaged."

He lifted his eyebrows. "Well, that's news to me. I've been keeping a wide berth from her because of her bad side, so it's totally possible.

He slipped his hand over mine, startling me. "I'm sorry she's not nicer to you." He moved his thumb across the palm of my hand, sending more tingles up my arm. After a few more seconds, I slipped my hand away.

"This is a lot to take in at once, you know? Why didn't you tell me this earlier?"

Cam shrugged and sat back against the couch, a little deflated. "If you knew you were dating your boss's ex, would you have even given me a chance?"

I shrugged. "I don't know. I mean, probably not."

He shifted next to me. "And this was why I was worried."

"I'm sorry."

Cam shook his head. "Don't be, but I'd really like to see *you* again."

I shook my head. "I just don't know if I can get any more involved with you than I already am. If Millie found out, she could fire me, and I'd lose the resort again."

His face fell a little, and he rose to his feet. "I understand. Really, I do. You've got to look out for yourself. I can't tell you what to do, but I can say listening to Millie has never been a good idea for me."

My heart seemed to sink, all of my lovely possibilities with this man slowly slipping away.

"Anyway, I better get to the hospital before the roads are closed."

There was something left that he wasn't ready to

talk about, but I could wait. I stood up as he put on his coat. He swung the door open, bringing in another gust of snow and wind. "I'll see you around, Rory."

Suddenly I didn't want him to go. Not now. The roads were bad, and we still hadn't figured anything out.

"Wait," I said, running after him. I followed him outside into the wet and cold. My bare feet protested as they were buried in a foot of icy snow. At least three more inches had fallen, and it wouldn't be stopping anytime soon. "Don't go," I said.

I grabbed for him as he started down the steps, then wrapped my arms around myself to hold in the heat. He paused, looking down at where my hand had been. Then he took off his coat and wrapped it around me.

"I understand you're hesitant to start anything that might enrage Millie even more. More than you know, I get it."

I looked up into his eyes as snowflakes kissed our eyelids. Why couldn't things just be easy with us? "I just need some time to think."

He smiled and stepped closer. "I can give you that."

A gut-wrenching feeling settled in the pit of my stomach. I didn't want him to go, and yet, I knew the risks of what I would be doing if I dated him. "Be careful driving."

He rubbed my shoulders and warmth spread down my back. "Don't worry about me. My truck is great in snow."

My teeth began to chatter as the snow soaked my feet. "Will you text me when you get to the hospital, so

I know you're okay?"

He pulled me in for a bear hug, and I couldn't help it—I snuggled into his warmth. Oh man, he smelled so good. Why did he have to be so . . . warm?

"So you at least care about me?" he said, grinning.

I pulled back and smirked. "I care if you hit a tree and die." That wasn't entirely true. There were feelings growing inside me, even if I wasn't sure what they meant.

He laughed. "Alright, alright. I'll text you when I'm safe."

I nodded and gave him back his coat. Snow and wet seeped into my clothes and stung at my feet, the cold wrapping around my bones. "Drive carefully."

He gave me a salute. "Yes, ma'am. I'll see you around, Rory."

And then he was gone. I watched his tires spin in the snow as he left, his tracks vanishing within seconds. It was as if he'd never been here.

Chapter 10

Cam never texted that night. And by morning, my phone still remained empty of any news from him. I tried to push the fearful feeling aside, knowing that he'd probably forgotten once he arrived at the hospital. Just in case, I sent him a lighthearted text to remind him of our joke yesterday.

Did you die or does hugging that tree feel too good?

But when he didn't reply after hours of waiting, I chalked it up to a busy day for him at the hospital. Instead of cleaning the house like I usually did on Saturdays, I sat by the window and watched the snow pile up on the side of the road while drinking a mug of cocoa. The snow plows rumbled past, throwing the snow to the side, only to have to return an hour later to repeat the process. The dirty slush piled higher and higher until it resembled a tall wall, blocking my view of the outside world, cocooning me in safety.

I tried to not think about Cam; I really did. But all I could remember was how his touch affected me. I'd be kidding myself if I said there was nothing there. I felt something. A spark of interest. Curiosity.

Even reading and watching TV wasn't enough to completely distract me. The phone stayed clutched in my hand all day. It was silly because I knew he wouldn't call. Doctors were busy, and why would he call? He'd already given me a gym pass, but I couldn't help but wish he had another reason to stop by. But then again, the secrets he kept inside scared me more than my attraction to him. By dinner time, I couldn't resist sending another text.

Please just text me back so I know you're okay.

And still no response. I couldn't send a third message after that, so I ended up turning off my phone and going to bed early, annoyed at how anxious I was.

When Sunday rolled around, I was going stir-crazy from staying inside all day. Rose called to invite me over for brunch, and I welcomed the invitation. Tall mounds of snow still lined either side of the street, but the temperatures were rising and the roads were clear.

Everything looked new and clean. Other than the curled-up slush pushed to the side, the snow was white and beautiful. The resort had been pumping in snow for weeks, and the cost of maintenance couldn't have made Millie very happy. Hopefully, she'd see this as a bright spot tomorrow.

The ninnies were bickering with each other by the time I opened the door and dropped my keys in the dish in the front entry hall. At least I never lost my keys there.

Mary's voice echoed from the kitchen. "Rose, you're going to burn this chili if you don't hurry up and get in here."

"Oh, hush, Mary. I just need this last herb." I heard sounds of her stretching to reach something and then a crash from inside their little greenhouse attached to the side of the kitchen. "Ah, I got it."

Rose came down the hallway toward me, carrying a plant pulled up at the root. She wore an old house dress, her hair pulled back in a tight bun. She rarely wore makeup since she had naturally rosy cheeks and lips and never seemed to age.

"Dill," Rose said, lifting the plant. "Perfect for chili and my secret ingredient," she sang, rubbing my arm as she passed. "Glad you decided to come, Rory. The others don't appreciate my cooking as much as you do."

I followed her into the kitchen and sat down on one of the kitchen stools.

"Finally," Mary said, passing Rose the spatula and moving away from the gas stove. Her cheeks were red, beads of sweat dripping down her face. She grabbed her medical journal and began to fan herself. "I'm getting hot flashes standing in front of this fire."

Dawn came waltzing into the room, snapping a picture of all three of us. "Lovely memories of our time together."

"Lovely indeed," Mary snapped, waving her journal at Dawn, but Dawn evaded her and took another one.

I smiled as they continued their fun and

sometimes cantankerous arguing.

"Girls, girls," Rose said. "I want to talk to Rory, not fuss with you."

The three turned to stare at me. I grabbed a celery stalk and a knife Rose had been eyeing and began cutting the stalk into tiny pieces on the cutting board. This wasn't my first chili rodeo. "Oh, I'm content sitting here and listening to you three bicker. It's one of my favorite noises."

Mary cackled, and I was reminded of how similar she was to a witch, one of the short, stubby ones with a sharp eye and a cranky disposition. Still, I loved her. "Have you heard about what happened to your doctor friend?"

Rose and Dawn stopped moving and glanced at me.

The knife wavered in my hand. "Heard about what? What happened to him?"

Rose glared at Mary across the room. "She's just wondered if you've seen him again."

Mary lifted her eyebrows but didn't contradict Rose.

I sighed. "Well, actually yes. We went skiing together the other night."

"Skiing?" Rose's face lit up. "You haven't been skiing since . . ." Her voice trailed off as she scrutinized my face.

"I know. It's okay. I even told Cam a little bit about Mom and Dad. He was really nice about everything. I'm just a little worried. He left my house during the peak of the snowstorm."

"And you haven't talked to him since then?" Mary asked, her brows coming together in one thick, bushy

95

line across her forehead.

I went back to cutting the celery. "No. He was supposed to text me when he made it to the hospital okay, but he hasn't. I'm sure everything's fine." But deep inside, I knew it wasn't fine. Doctors were busy, but this was ridiculous. Sending an "I got here safely" message took less than thirty seconds.

"I'm sure things are fine and he's just been busy at the hospital," Rose said sweetly.

The four of us settled into our tasks, and, after the ingredients were added, we watched the antiques roadshow program on Netflix while the chili simmered. Throughout the show, I kept checking my phone to see if he'd replied.

"She's checking that thing a lot," Dawn said, poking Mary.

"I am not." I threw the phone down.

"Do you have other plans tonight, dearie? We're perfectly okay with sending you home with a bowl of chili."

I shook my head. "Uh, no, you're not getting rid of me that easily. Plus one bowl is never enough, and you know that."

Rose's pale cheeks turned a rosy pink. "Aw, shucks, Rory. I do love that you adore my cooking. I think the chili is ready."

Cam was forgotten as we stuffed our faces. They sent me home with a large Tupperware of chili an hour later, and I was glad I'd have a few hours to decompress before going back to sleep.

When I pulled down my street, a navy-blue truck that looked suspiciously like Cam's was parked a few houses away from mine. My heart fluttered in my

chest. When I pulled in, he was leaning against my garage. What did he want?

The fading sun shone on him at just the right angle to light up his whole face. He had on a pair of jeans and a white, long-sleeved T-shirt with a baseball logo. Where was his jacket? Wasn't he cold?

His smile grew as I climbed out of the car and waved. Stopping a foot away from him, I crossed my arms.

"Why didn't you text me back that you were okay? I was worried."

His eyebrows lifted. "I don't even have my phone. I lost it during my shift last night."

Relief washed over me. "So you're still interested?"

He smirked. "Yeah, I'm definitely interested." He stepped a little closer and reached for my hand, staring down at it as he twined his fingers with mine. "I'm just wondering how you're feeling . . . about us?"

His hands were freezing in mine. I rubbed at them instinctively. Waiting for him to contact me all weekend had been a pretty good sign that I was ready to pursue this. "I'm definitely interested. I just don't know how much."

He smiled widely. "I'll take it."

"Aren't you cold?" I said, rubbing his fingers. They hadn't warmed up any.

He looked down at his bare arms. "Oh, yeah a bit, but I can't stay long anyway."

Now it was my turn to frown.

"Sorry. This is the first moment I've been able to get away since arriving at the hospital. They called me in the moment I stepped through the doors. I'm finally taking a short break after a twenty-four hour shift.

Anyway, I'm okay."

So he hadn't forgotten me. "You could've called. You didn't need to drive all—"

"I needed to see you."

He *needed* to see me? His bluntness continued to surprise me. "Uh, why?"

"To make sure—" Cam's attention focused behind me, and I twisted around to see what he was looking at. It was Mrs. Johnson walking her dog. She'd been neighbors with our family since I was a baby.

"Hey, Rory," she said, her voice coming out in breathy fog. She walked in place as Rufus found a new spot to mark, her jogging suit swishing as she moved. "How's the resort doing? I haven't had a chance to make it up the big hill yet."

"Hey, everything is great," I lied. "We're keeping busy."

I stepped back to where Cam was so I could introduce him, but he wasn't behind me. I whipped around and searched the driveway. I saw him walking to his truck with his beeper in his hand. Was he leaving?

Rubbing the back of my neck, I turned back to finish up my conversation with Mrs. Johnson before Cam left. "It looks like you're keeping busy yourself. Thanks for saying hi."

She didn't get the hint and continued talking. "You know, Mr. Johnson is doing well. He loves being retired, and we've been able to fit in a lot of traveling. In fact, next month, we're going to Wyoming. And after that, we'll be going to Europe to visit my uncle for the first time in ten years."

I fidgeted with the zipper on my jacket as she

continued to drone on and on about vacation plans. I kept an eye on the truck, not wanting him to leave without the chance to finish our talk. Why did Mrs. Johnson have to talk so much? I wrapped my arms around myself, hoping to sell what I was about to say.

"Well, it was good to see you. I better get inside. I've got company."

She looked behind me, her eyebrows coming together in a hard line. "You do? I didn't see anyone."

I turned to make sure the truck was still there. "Yep, he's just on a call. But I better get inside."

"Okay, honey," she said, as if I were a child.

I rolled my eyes. She and the other older neighbors thought I was going to break any second.

She gave me a sympathetic smile and came closer to pat my cheek. "I worry about you being here all alone. We sure miss your parents."

I dropped my hands. Guilt creeped in as Mrs. Johnson's eyes filled with concern. She had been one of Mom's friends. "Thanks. I'm doing well."

After a long, uncomfortable hug, Mrs. Johnson walked her dog down the street and around the corner. Only seconds later, I heard Cam's footsteps behind me.

"Sorry I bailed."

I whipped around. "Why did you disappear? I wanted to introduce you to my neighbor. She's always worried about me being lonely, but I swear she didn't believe me when I said I had company."

He looked to where Mrs. Johnson disappeared behind the corner. "Hmm."

"So was it the hospital?" I added, when he didn't add why he'd left.

"Yeah, it was. They paged me."

"Didn't you lose your phone?"

"Yeah, I snagged one of the loaner phones from work. Anyway, I haven't slept in a while, and the hospital might need me for another shift soon. I've got to get back."

Disappointment seeped in as my questions threatened to spill out of my mouth. "Well, thanks for stopping by, I guess."

He wiped his hand across his face, his stubble longer than normal. He looked cute with a little facial hair. "The next few days might be crazy at the hospital. Look, I need you to do something for me."

"Sure, anything," I said.

Cam threw a side glance at me. Was that a nervous look in his eyes? "I need you to talk to Jasmine."

"Okay, what's up? Does she need to talk?"

He shook his head. "She'll know what to say. Just call her. Please."

"Okay, I will."

Cam hesitated another second, squeezing my hand once more. Then he headed back to his truck.

I sighed. At least now I knew he was safe.

I called Jasmine as soon as I went inside, leaning on the couch and shivering as her phone rang and rang before finally taking me to voicemail.

After I listened to a short and upbeat "I'm not here right now, I'll call you back", I left what I hoped wasn't an ominous message.

"Hey, Jasmine. Just checking in. Give me a call back when you have a minute."

I hung up the phone and headed to the bathroom

for a hot shower. I wasn't sure why Cam wanted me to call Jasmine, but I had plenty to think about as I washed the cold away from my body.

I had to decide if dating Cam meant putting my job at risk.

Chapter 11

On Monday morning, the front desk called for me as soon as I signed in to my computer.

"Rory, we need to talk," Mrs. Jessie said through the intercom. Instead of her usual enthusiasm, her voice sounded clipped and sharp.

I rolled my eyes. One guess as to whom this was about. "Be right there." I stopped what I was doing and headed down to the main lobby.

True to my suspicion, they didn't want to discuss anything. "Since she won't come down here, and she refuses to let us come up for an in-person meeting, please take this note to Her Majesty," Mr. Jessie said, his arms crossed firmly across his chest. He gave me a small smile, and I knew that his anger was not targeted at me. But then the smile melted away. "And please let her know we need an in-person answer."

I gulped. This was sure to ruin whatever good

feelings Millie had today. "Sure thing."

I took my time taking the stairs to her office. I read the message on the way up, knowing what was written already. They were unhappy with Millie's lack of involvement in the resort's affairs. Mr. and Mrs. Jessie weren't exactly quiet about their complaints. But they knew the ins and outs of the resort, and Millie would be shooting herself in the foot to fire them.

I watched my Fitbit tick off the steps I walked. It helped give me the gumption I needed to deliver the message. I folded the note back up and walked out of the stairwell and down the hall to her office.

I could hear her voice from halfway down the hall. I bit my lip as I thought of how best to interrupt whatever business she was taking care of. A loud male voice boomed within the office as I approached. "You let me down."

I peeked in. A familiar man with wide shoulders and wearing a black suit stood at the window. Millie stood in front of him, facing the mountain while his glare remained on her.

I knew him. *Mr. Perez.* How could I forget his face? And Millie *Perez.* How did I not put that together before this? My heart stirred as I remembered signing the resort over to him. Since it was still in my name, and I had no blood relatives that I knew of, I had been the one required to sign the paperwork.

Instead of showing compassion, he was unequivocally disinterested in what he was taking over. And now, finding out Millie was related to him somehow made so much sense why we hadn't connected more. She was as mean as her dad.

"Millie, are you listening to me?" he snapped, his voice making me jump. She seemed to wilt as he demanded a reply.

"It's not my fault, Dad. I tried to make things work between us, and now . . ." She put her face in her hands and sobbed.

So he is *her dad.* I felt a twinge of sympathy for her as he stared down at her with malicious eyes. Wait, that meant he must know Cam too. Was this why Cam wanted out of the business relationship?

"What do I do now?" she said, her voice small and weak.

Mr. Perez lowered his arms and cracked his fingers menacingly. "If he can't be coerced into doing what's right for the resort, maybe I'll just have to get involved myself."

I perked up at his words. Were they talking about Cam? If this involved him, I needed to give him a heads up.

Millie huffed. "My life is not one of your deals, Daddy." She said his name bitterly. At least she was trying to put up a fight.

Pity for Millie flooded through me. No wonder she had been so emotional lately. I stared at my side of the door, debating whether or not I should come back later.

"You'll do as you're told," Mr. Perez said, gritting his teeth and chucking her chin. "We'll talk about this later. It looks like you have someone waiting for you, and, more than anything, you need to keep doing your job."

Millie's head snapped to the door. She gave me the glare she reserved just for me, but I was too worried Mr. Perez would recognize me as he passed. If he did notice me, he didn't show any signs we'd met before. I sighed in relief. Millie didn't need to know any more about me than she already did.

"Rory!" Millie snapped. "Do you make it a habit of eavesdropping on others' private conversations?"

With you? Always. I looked up to see her fuming in my direction with uneven smoky eyes. *Oh, I should've run.*

"What do you want?" Her voice was edgy and mean, but I tried to remember all she was going through.

I clasped my hands together, trying to hide the note. "It was nothing. Just checking on you. Do you need anything?"

She hadn't stopped glaring. "No. Why would I ever—" Her attention settled on my hands. "What's that? Do you have a message?"

I looked down to see the little paper wedged between two fingers. *Drat.* "Yeah, it's nothing. The front desk sent me with a message, but if you're busy, I'll just take care of it."

"Read it to me," she demanded.

"Are . . . Are you sure? Mr. and Mrs. Jessie seemed pretty upset, and I don't know if you want me to kn—"

"Read it to me or get out. Your choice."

Leaving sounded like the better idea, but her interpretation of 'get out' was probably different than mine. "Yes. Okay. Here it is." I unfolded the paper and started reading.

"So you've stooped to writing emails to check in with us. You want to know how your hotel is doing?" I paused and looked down so I wouldn't have to meet

105

her eyes. "Maybe I shouldn't be the one—"

"Finish the letter, you weanie."

My face flushed with heat. All I was trying to do was save her the embarrassment and the extra heartache. If she wanted it, here it was. The paper shook as I continued to read. "How about instead of asking how we're doing at our jobs, you walk the 100 steps to the front office and talk to us face to face. You're General Manager, which means you should be concerned about all areas of this resort. How about you do your job?"

When I looked up from the letter, Millie's eyes were stony, staring straight ahead without looking at anything. She turned away and dismissed me with her hand. "You can go now."

The sympathetic side of me kicked in. "It's actually 154 steps," I said, correcting the note. "What do the front desk people know anyway?" *I mean, other than everything.* But taking sides against Millie would only put me in boiling water as well. If Mr. and Mrs. Jessie still had a job by the end of the day, I'd be surprised.

She tapped the desk with her hand. Her empty hand. Where was her ring?

"Your ring is missing?" The words fell out of my mouth before I could stop them. Putting a hand over my lips, I began to apologize. "Sorry, I know it's not my business, but I am here to help you too. If I can make anything easier . . ."

Millie glanced down at her bare hand, then ripped it off the desk, hiding under the table. "I was . . . He's in a . . ." Her face continued to twist in distress, and she stumbled to find words.

106

I backed toward the door. "I shouldn't have said anything. I just wanted you to know I'm here. If you need anything." I gave a weak laugh. "I can even plan an event, just to cheer you up."

She swiveled in her chair and stared out the big, glass window in her office, which overlooked Black Diamond Hill. I kept moving toward the door, but before I could make my silent exit, she whipped around, her eyes full of something new. Hope maybe? Excitement?

"I guess he wouldn't care," she said, her eyes growing bigger. "There's a good chance he won't remember anyway."

"Who won't remember?"

She snapped her fingers together. "I-I have to go. Tell the receptionists I will meet with them tomorrow afternoon. Cancel my appointments for today. Then take care of the Trekis Corporation coming this afternoon for their lunch training meeting. Everything's already set to go. A dummy could run that event."

I dug my fingernails into my side. I was the one who'd arranged the event, so of course, I could run it.

"Wipe that look off your face, Rory. We don't have room in here for your ego. Tomorrow morning, you and Brittney meet me at 8:00 sharp. We have a new event to book, and we'll need to get started right away."

"A new event? Wait, wh—"

"Since when do you ask so many questions? Do your job." A slow smile started across her face.

Whatever she was planning, I knew I wasn't going to like it.

After work, I stared at my gym bag on the passenger seat of my car. I'd hastily packed it this morning as an afterthought, shoving my badge inside last of all. Just in case. I did have a really good excuse to talk to Cam if I happened to see him. He should know that the Perezes were planning something. Even if I didn't know what that something was, I could at least warn him. And the sooner I began my marathon training, the better.

Yep, no more excuses. I started the car and headed to the hospital.

As I drove, I daydreamed about running into Cam. A small part of me wanted to see him again. His voice, his laugh, his hand over mine. But he'd also dated Millie. I didn't know much about dating, but what could he have seen in her?

Up until now, my relationships had epically failed. There were Brandon and Devin in high school, who were fun and exciting but too immature to make a relationship work. And after two years of dating Joseph in college, he found having only one girl on his arm wasn't enough. Even if I didn't date Cam, something inside me was finally ready to take that next step with someone. I had been single long enough.

I drove around to the back side of the hospital and parked. A small reception area was just inside the door, but instead of a line, a plump, white-haired lady gestured me forward. She had a round face, a whole bunch of wrinkles, and kind eyes. "What can I help you with, dear?"

I smiled at her. Why hadn't she been at the front desk the other day? "This is my first time to the gym." I pulled out my pass and handed it to her.

"Ah, yes. It's on the basement floor, down the hallway from the cafeteria. Though why they put a gym near food is beyond me. If I had my choice..." She threw up her hands and rolled her eyes.

I laughed. *What a cute grandma she must be.* "Good point. I'll plug my nose on my way."

She was still laughing as I made my way to the elevator. I clicked the down button and waited. A doctor passed, but otherwise the hallways were empty.

Finally, the doors pinged open with a whoosh. I stepped inside and stopped short. Cam leaned against the far wall of the elevator, frowning, with his arms crossed.

"Cam, what are *you* doing down here?" I almost laughed as I heard the words coming out of my mouth. He had more reason to be here than I did.

"Did you call Jasmine?" he asked quickly.

I nodded. "I did, but she didn't answer. I left a message but she didn't call back."

His eyes were smoky blue as they studied me. "Will you try again? Please?"

I raised my eyebrows and waited until the door closed. "Yes. But can't you tell me why? What's going on?"

He shook his head. "I couldn't explain it if I tried. Just please, call her."

"Okay, I'll try again," I said. I felt like calling her right then just to know what he looked so worried about. Was this about her and Joe? Did she need relationship advice?

"So what are you doing here then?" he asked.

Remembering I was in a closed elevator that hadn't moved yet, I hit the basement button. "I'm heading to the gym. You know, to use the pass you gave me? To start training."

Cam dropped his hands and stood in front of the door. "Oh, I'll come with you then."

"You're not busy?"

He ran a hand through his hair. "I have some time to kill." The elevator door pinged open, and he led the way.

"By the way, the Perezes are planning something, so heads up."

He looked back at me, slowing down to match my stride. "They always are. That's why we're not in business together anymore."

Three nurses came toward us, laughing and talking loudly. They looked younger than me and plenty confident. They were all blond and reminded me of cheerleaders from high school. As we passed each other, the nurse on the end closest to Cam seemed to walk right through him, pushing him to the side and out of the way.

Cam's face went pale, and he stopped moving.

They had done that on purpose! I whipped around, the adrenaline rushing through my body. "Why don't you watch where you're going?"

The three of them stopped and turned around. The shortest one lifted an eyebrow. "Are you okay?"

Her tone of voice set me off even more. I wasn't crazy. "No, you just don't push people aside."

The one in the middle, who had a tattoo showing

110

under the edge of her sleeve, shook her head. "We didn't even touch you."

I opened my mouth, then closed it when I saw Cam. He had plastered himself against the wall. His eyes were scrunched tightly together. "Hey, are you okay?" I said to him.

The nurses stalked off, mumbling something about the mental wing of the hospital, but I was too worried to care.

I shook Cam's shoulder softly. "You look as white as . . . well, your jacket."

Cam gave a grim smile. "Yeah, just thrown off guard."

I pointed a thumb behind me. "Can you believe them? It's like they walked right through you. Did you make them mad or something?"

Cam straightened. "Let's go," he looked toward the gym doors a few feet away, "in there."

"That's where I *was* going," I mumbled, grabbing the door and flinging it open. I gasped as I took the room in: a smaller running track and a glassed-in area for fitness classes. "Wow, this is amazing. There are a lot of people up there."

Cam pointed to the track. "Yep, and no one really uses the track. Let's go warm up over there." He pointed to a spot in the corner. "You need to stretch."

I narrowed my eyes. "I thought you didn't want me here?"

He ignored my jab and walked over next to a set of bleachers, hiding him from view. I reluctantly followed. He took off his jacket and patted the floor next to him. "Time to warm up."

He taught me a few stretches, and I tried not to

111

act self-conscious as I stretched in front of him. He didn't seem to pay much attention to me anyway. His eyes were on the track and whenever someone came near us, he stiffened.

"Is everything okay? You look kind of unfocused."

He laughed. "It's just been a weird few days, that's all." He stood and led a few standing stretches, bending to each side and to the middle.

I followed his every movement, making sure my backside was always away from him.

During one of our stretches, he said, "Tell me about work. I mean, I know you're something other than Millie's assistant."

I rolled my eyes. "Yeah, I'm supposed to be. I really wanted this job so I could plan events. I love when groups come to the resort and grow closer together through team-building activities. For some of them, it's their first time skiing, and that's always fun to see." I gritted my teeth, remembering the injustice of what my position was supposed to be compared to what it really was. "But Millie keeps me hidden a lot of the time, making me dust lampshades and other things she thinks our cleaning crew is incapable of doing. And then you know, sometimes I get to run errands to the hospital where I have to convince people to sign ridiculous papers."

"Well, for my sake, I'm glad it was you, not her, that showed up that day."

I gave him a tentative smile in return. "I just hope one day Millie notices my wide range of skills and uses me as more than just her slave."

"Well, maybe you were made to do something better. Away from Ski Ridge."

"I like being close to my parents."

Cam stopped stretching and stood up. "If Millie doesn't treat you well, it's not worth it."

I rolled my shoulders back. "Millie isn't nice to anyone. I don't take it personally."

"Touché." He chuckled and moved onto the track, and I followed with some hesitancy. Was he going to make me run a mile today? Because that wouldn't go over well.

"The key to long-distance running is that you have to pace yourself. People with the goal to run a marathon before a certain age—"

"Like me," I interjected.

He chuckled. "Like you, well, they approach it all wrong. They think that running long distances the first week will get them back in shape. But chances are, more than half of those people are out of shape, not regular runners, and could seriously injure themselves by being too eager."

"So we're going to walk then?" This plan sounded better already.

"Kind of. You're going to have to commit to walking or running most days. Are you good with that?"

"Yeah, sure. I can stop by on my way home every day."

He paused. "You know, today was a rare day for me not to be working. Sometimes, I can meet you down here at the same time, but I hope you won't come looking for me."

And the tactless beast has returned. "Geez, I won't bug you, okay."

"I didn't mean it like that. I just—" He sighed, and

113

I noticed the bags under his eyes. He must not be getting much sleep.

"It's okay." I pressed a hand to his arm. He looked down at it, then took my hand in his.

"Sorry, I'm just under a lot of stress right now at the hospital." He dropped my hand and nodded toward the track. "Now about this; we're going to start at a fast walk, and then jog, then walk again. You're used to walking fast, so this shouldn't be so hard."

I lifted an eyebrow. "You've watched me?"

"Well, yeah. You're kind of hard not to notice."

Heat filled my cheeks. "Um, thanks."

"You're welcome." His confident smile wavered.

"Have you thought more about us and where you think this is going?" he said, pointing to the two of us.

I blushed. I had thought about it, too much actually. "I guess if Millie has moved on, why shouldn't you? And it's not like I'm breaking any friend codes by dating her ex. Maybe taking it slow would be good though."

He smiled, sending warmth down the length of my spine. "Slow is good."

I smiled too. We were really doing this.

He turned to the track. I followed his gaze. An older couple entered the track from the other side, holding hands and beginning their circuit.

"Time to get going. I'm going to walk at a fast pace. Try not to talk. The key to a good running schedule is to have some variation. Do a light jog, then a brisk walk on breaks. If you feel like slowing down, do it, but don't stop."

The couple came around the corner toward us.

He nodded toward the track. "Let's go ahead of them a little bit. Ready?"

I nodded and followed a little ways behind him. I almost laughed, since he wasn't dressed for running at all. Slacks, a long shirt, and some business shoes. Not exactly running getup. But somehow, he made it look effortless.

He started off with a brisk walk, and I boogied after him just to keep up. After a few minutes, he started running, and my stress level picked up. But before I could get comfortable with the speed, he had slowed down to his brisk walk again.

I breathed as quietly as I could, not wanting him to hear me pant like a dog. By the time we had completed our first mile, I was dripping in sweat. The only thing that kept me going as he started the second mile was that, right in front of me, I had the very best view.

Chapter 12

"O uch," I said, wincing as I climbed out of the car the next morning. I reached over and grabbed my stuff, balancing Millie's coffee, my keys, and my purse. Every step felt like I was dragging weight behind me. We'd only done three miles yesterday, but it reminded me why I hadn't taken the next step to actually start running. There were people who *walked* the entire lengths of marathons, right?

My phone rang, and I shoved the keys into my purse to free up my hands. Had Jasmine finally called me back? I had left one more voicemail and a text message last night.

But it was Brittney whose name lit up the screen.

"Hey, I'm back," she sang into the phone. "Just walking in right now. Did you survive without me?"

I walked as fast as my sore legs would let me, shifting the phone to my shoulder so I could open the door. "Um, actually, yesterday was weird, and you need to head to Millie's." I caught Brittney up on yesterday's conversation with Millie, including the bit about her dad owning the resort and that she had a new event coming up.

"What's the event?" Brittney asked.

"She didn't say what it would be, but she seemed really excited about it. You know how when the villain shows their soft side, and you think they've changed? Then they rip your head off?"

She was silent for a few seconds. "Which one will she be this morning?"

I sighed as I saw her waiting at the door of Millie's office. "Probably the softened villain."

Brittney studied her nails as I approached. "Maybe it won't be so bad. You worry too much."

I smirked at her. "Hmm, well, don't hold your breath." I lifted the coffee cup in my hand. "Although I've got her coffee, so maybe you're right. Can't slap the hand that caffeinates you."

I eyed her ensemble. She wore a bright-green blouse, a jean skirt, and green lipstick to match her top. Her braids were back, and little red ribbons were woven through them. "You look ready for Christmas," I said, laughing. "Millie is going to get you for your lipstick. Here." I pulled out a tissue from my purse, but she refused it.

"She never cares about my lips." Brittney looked down at my shoes. "But I bet you won't get away with those shoes."

I looked down at my outfit. My new tennis shoes, a pair of new jeans, and a nice blouse. "If she yells at me about my shoes and ignores your lipstick, I'll buy you lunch."

Brittney laughed. "You're on."

Millie's face appeared around the corner, making the both of us jump. Her eyelashes were extra thick today, the spiders back for another attack on her face.

"Why are my two assistants chittering outside my office like little squirrels? There's work to do. Get in here."

When she turned her back, I smirked at Brittney. There was no way Millie would miss her lipstick.

Brittney and I sat down in the two stiff chairs facing her desk. But instead of sitting across from us, Millie stood over her desk, watching us with beady, black eyes. I scooted her coffee over to her, but she ignored it.

"I called you two in here this morning because we have a new event to plan that will change how we do things around here for a while."

Brittney looked my way, but I kept my eyes trained on Millie.

"In the last few months, Rory has taken every order I've given her and performed it to the best of her ability, although her ability needs some work." I opened my mouth, but she held up her hand. "Sorry. Now's not the time. We have too much to do."

"So, how are things going to change?" Brittney asked, twirling a piece of her hair.

Millie clapped her hands. "Well, this is the exciting part. Brittney, I'm going to need Rory for my special project, so I will need you to take care of all operating events. They're planned for a month in advance. When there's nothing to do, you can call old clients and make new events. But basically keep the ship running."

Calling old clients was not effective. Emailing them would be a much better use of her time. I pressed my lips together. She was handing Brittney what I had wanted since coming here and on a silver platter to boot. "Congrats, Brittney." My voice wavered, and the words sounded fake, even to me. "Good thing she wore your lucky new lipstick, right, Millie?"

Millie glanced at her for half a second. "Yeah, looks great."

Brittney grinned wide. "Thanks, boss."

I sighed in exasperation. This was so unfair.

"Aw, now don't be sad, Rory," Millie said. "I saved the best for last. I have an event happening that will be a show-stopper for this resort. People will hear about it and book the resort for future, similar events."

What could I possibly be doing that would trump running all the events at the resort? That was the closest I could get to my dream job right now, and she'd given free rein to Brittney—who picked the easy way out every time. And wore green lipstick to work.

Sitting up straighter, I waited for the nail in my coffin. "Well, I'm happy to help. What is it that we're going to be doing?"

Millie's smile grew. "Before I tell you what it is, I need you to agree to some stipulations."

I glanced toward Brittney, who arched one of her already high eyebrows. "Okay," I said. Was there really a choice at this point?

Millie grabbed a folder from her desk and held it tightly to her chest. "First of all, Rory, this event has

119

got to be planned by you. My attendance will be spotty in the next few weeks, so you'll have to bring your A-game."

At least this part sounded good. Less Millie. More planning. "Okay, I can do that."

Millie's face twitched. "This event has a time limit. Thirty-four days, to be exact, and we are already four days into that time limit."

I coughed to make sure I had heard right. "Thirty-four days?"

"Yep, and everything has to be perfect, because the whole state of California will be watching. I did tell you my dad was a bigwig in his area of business, right? He owns over thirty properties."

I flinched. *He is also the heartless buyer of my parents' business.* "Uh, no, but what does that have to do with anything?"

Millie took a seat and opened the file. "Before I tell you, I need to know if you're okay with everything so far."

Less than two months? I already felt the anxiety building in my chest. Events usually took months to plan. I'd have to work non-stop. Late hours, long weekends, maybe even bring my work home. I shuddered. What was I getting myself into?

"I'll sweeten the deal a bit," she said. "If you pull this off, I will leave you and your events alone, and you can run this department the way you've wanted to do it."

I dropped my jaw. Was she kidding? I looked toward Brittney, and she gave me an encouraging smile. If I could make this happen, I would finally be doing my job without the weight of Millie's influence.

And if I didn't pull it off, well, at least I wouldn't be any worse off than I was already. "Yes," I blurted before I could change my mind. "Yes, I'll do it."

Millie smiled down at us and pulled the folder closer to her. "Okay, well as long as you don't wear those tennis shoes to work anymore, you've got the job."

Brittney looked over at me, a smug expression on her face. I wanted to point out the alien green clinging to her lips, but there were more pressing matters.

"I know you are more than capable of pulling this off," Millie continued. I didn't really believe that. More than likely, she was simply desperate. There was no other reason for her to give me this much responsibility. She opened the folder and slid it over.

Brittney and I moved forward at the same time. Pictures of floral arrangements, table centerpieces, and men in tuxedos spilled out as the folder glided toward us. My mind whirled as I looked at each picture, the possibilities buzzing in my head. A prom maybe? Or an anniversary? I gasped as I reached the final picture. A girl in a wedding dress.

"Am I planning a wedding?" We had never held a wedding at the resort, but Millie was right. If I pulled this off, it would be the launch of new events booked at the resort. Our business would skyrocket.

Millie nodded. "Yes, you are."

"Well that's awesome. I've never done it, but I doubt it will be any different than most other events. We need flowers, a cake, and centerpieces." All of the possibilities popped into my head at once, fighting for my attention.

"Well, whose wedding is it? Who's the client?"

Brittney asked, a hint of jealousy in her tone.

Millie snagged the edge of the file and slid it toward me. She pulled out a picture from inside her desk and added it to the top of the stack.

I dropped my jaw. No, no, no. This couldn't be happening. There was no pleasing *this* client.

Millie's smile turned mischievous. "Oh, yes. The client who is hiring you to plan their wedding is me."

Chapter 13

"What's your return policy?" I tapped my finger against the phone as I waited for the florist's reply. Finding flowers for the event was my first responsibility, and already, three florists had turned me down.

He laughed wryly. "For a wedding that needs to happen in less than two months, I'd say there isn't one."

"How about exchanges?" My heart hammered. *Please let me book at least one thing on the list to show I'm not completely incompetent.*

"Uh, probably not. Make sure your bride really wants the flowers you're ordering. They'll be extra if I have to ship them from somewhere else."

I narrowed my eyes. Obviously, he hadn't ever worked for a bridezilla, or a Millie-zilla as Brittney and I referred to her in the privacy of our office. But, he was the last florist within an hour's drive. "Okay, book me for that date, and I'll get back to you with the specifics."

He chuckled. "Okay, don't take your time. If you want it by—"

"Yeah, I know." I slammed my office phone down and glared across the desk.

Brittney sat in her chair, eating an apple and smiling at me. "Well, at least you've got one thing booked."

Putting my head down on the cool desk, I allowed myself a moment to close my eyes. Life at work had been a whirlwind since she had assigned me her wedding two days ago, and I barely had enough time to shove bites of food into my mouth between calls. Tonight, I wanted so badly to go in and continue my running schedule, but it was impossible with how late I'd be working.

I was a little sad Cam hadn't contacted me at all. Or maybe I was too busy to notice if he'd even tried. I would have loved to see him. Being with him was a new comfort, and I really needed that.

I sighed and got down to business, calling any and all cake makers in the area. At least Millie would be gone more than usual. She told us she had personal issues to attend to, and everything she wanted was in the folder.

But on the rare moments when she came in to check on plans, she micro-managed me to the point where I was afraid to make a decision.

"Rory, there you are. Are you sleeping in here?" Millie's voice snapped me out of my daydream. Her eyes looked less lashy but her lids were heavy with lavender eyeshadow. It probably would have looked nice if it hadn't looked drawn on by a five-year-old.

I stood, ramrod straight. "Sorry, just taking a breather." I sped right on through, giving her no time to yell. "I just booked a florist at Flowers on Main, and he's sure he can import the lilies you want in time. You're sure you want lilies?"

Millie stared down at her manicured nails. "Yes, order the amount I indicated in the file."

I dug my nails into my legs. That file was as helpful as Brittney was on a bad day. "Fine, I'll do that. Now, about your menu options. You said you wanted a choice of three meats. Is steak, salmon, and crab okay?"

Millie dropped her purse on Brittney's desk with a flop. "Phillip hates fish. Actually, no. He has an obsession with fish. He just won't eat them."

I picked up the file and scrambled through the mess of papers I still needed to organize. "Did you—"

"Write that in the file? Yes, Rory. What am I? An idiot?" Millie grabbed her purse, slinging it over her arm so fast that it barely missed Brittney's face. "I'm out of the office until next week. I want to see major progress by then."

"Next week? But how will I— Can I call you?"

Millie whirled around. "Absolutely not. If you're not capable of planning this event, Brittney would love this opportunity."

Brittney shook her head, her gold, glitter lipstick shining as she moved. But of course, Millie didn't notice.

I crossed my arms protectively across my chest. "I'll do it. I'll handle it."

Millie spun on her heel and headed for the door. "That's what I thought."

I held my breath as I waited until the sound of her heel clicks were far enough away that she couldn't possibly overhear me.

"See what you did?" Brittney asked, interrupting the pity party I was having in my head. "You got her all riled up."

My face burned red. "Excuse me?"

Brittney's smile faltered. "I was kidding, Rory. You didn't do anything. If anything you've done too much for that old witch."

Layers of anxiety settled in my stomach, and I felt like puking. There was too much to do. How was I going to get it done in twenty-six days? "I don't know what I'm doing. What if I plan this wedding, and she hates it?"

She turned to me. "Rory, if that girl isn't happy with all the effort you put into this event, then she deserves an unhappy wedding. Poor Phillip."

I shrugged. "You know, it's funny. I've looked through this file a hundred times, and I haven't seen much about Phillip. What does he want? What are his tux measurements? It's all a little weird."

"Maybe she's planning a fake wedding."

I laughed. "Yeah, I doubt it. No one goes through this much effort for nothing. And she's pulling out all the stops. She even gave me her black American Express."

Brittney shrugged. "All I know is that you can only do your best. And if she doesn't like it, the worst thing she could do is fire you. Would it really be such a horrible thing to be far away from this place?"

I pictured my parents up on the hill, sledding down, laughing and holding hands. This was the only place I felt close to them. My parents would want me to be happy, and right now, I wasn't.

"Yeah, I guess you're right."

Brittney scooted her chair next to mine. "Alright then, let's plan this wedding your way."

Chapter 14

Even though my legs felt like lead and my back ached from sitting at a desk all day, I stopped at the gym on my way home. I went in through the back, changed in a bathroom, and joined the dozen or so people already using the track. Most were walkers, but a few seemed to be experienced long-distance runners.

Cam was nowhere in sight. I couldn't help feeling a little disappointed. He made the time go a little bit faster. And when he sped ahead of me, it was a very distracting view.

I took his advice and intermittently ran and walked for three miles. By the end, I was sweaty and uncomfortable, but I felt good. If I couldn't go running every day, I would try for this every other day.

I grabbed my keys and the bag of clothes I'd hidden under the bleachers, then headed for the door.

When I opened it, Cam stood there, smiling at me.

"Hey!" he said. "Haven't seen you for a while. I thought you gave up on running."

My heartbeat quickened as I got closer. He looked so nice, and I looked so not. "Nope, I've just been busy. This is the first time I've had a chance. And before you ask, no, Jasmine has not called me back. Every time I try, it sends me straight to voicemail."

He raised his eyebrows. "Hmm, maybe see if you can track down Joe's number at work."

I shrugged. "I could try."

He nodded. "Good. I've been pretty busy myself," he said, leading the way down the hall. "Maybe we can hang out tonight. I'm leaving in a bit. Maybe we can talk about if your interest has increased."

My muscles tightened. I still didn't have a definite answer. Would he stop waiting if I didn't make a decision? My phone buzzed with a text. I held up my index finger for him to wait, then checked the message, in case it was Millie. I sighed in relief when I saw it was from Rose.

Lasagna in thirty if you want to come. Bring a guest if you want.

How timely. My eyes narrowed, and I looked around. Was Mary watching me? Had she called Rose? Mary worked on the third floor of the hospital, so it would be a crazy odd chance if she'd gone to the gym while I was here. At least if I brought him, Cam and Mary would have something to talk about, which would reduce potential awkwardness.

"Something good?" He gestured to the phone.

I slipped it back into my bag. "Actually, it was from some family friends. They invited me for lasagna

129

and happen to make the best food this city has to offer. Want to come along?"

Cam lifted an eyebrow. "Mmm, I love lasagna, but I'm going to ask for a raincheck."

I frowned. "Didn't you just say—"

"Oh, I do want to hang out. I forgot I need to run upstairs and check on a patient. Can we meet at your house in an hour?"

Suspicion grew in the back of my mind, but I pushed it away. "Sure, do you want me to save you some food?"

His eyes said yes, but he shook his head. "Thank you, but I'd better not."

"Your loss."

He winked and then spun on his heel.

My insides tingled with excitement. Instead of feeling exhausted, I was energized.

❄ ❄ ❄

I walked out to the front entry hall and grabbed my keys. All three ninnies bumbled behind me, concern touching the edges of their eye crinkles.

"Are you sure you can't stay?" Rose asked, a Tupperware full of lasagna leftovers held out toward me. "You've only been here a short time."

Dinner had been good, but I was too nervous to eat much. "Yeah, I need to take a shower. I feel gross."

"Do you want me to pack up some food for your date too?" Dawn asked.

The keys slipped from my hands. "How'd you—"

"Honey, you've been smiling since the moment you walked in here," Rose said, brushing my hair to the side. "I'm just surprised you didn't tell us. Who is it?"

I hid a smile behind my hand. "It's Cam. We've hung out a few times in the last few weeks. He's preparing me for a 5K and then maybe a marathon, if I can manage it."

Mary raised her bushy eyebrows, making them join together across her forehead. "You saw him? Today?"

"Yeah. He's meeting me at the house in thirty minutes."

"Mmm," the other ninnies said.

I rolled my eyes. "You three are doing it again. Acting weird. It's a good thing he didn't come with me."

"Oh, I'm sure we'll meet him soon enough," Rose said.

I froze. "Really? What do you know?"

Rose clamped her mouth together, and the three of them started pushing me toward the door.

Again? There was enough mystery in my life. Bracing my hands on either side of the door, I stopped the steamroll. "Why are you three keeping secrets from me? Out of all the people in my life—"

Rose stepped forward and pulled me in for a hug. I resisted for only a few seconds. "Honey, we don't know anything. But we're wildly good guessers, and we have to let things play out in their own time."

I pushed away. A sly grin touched the edges of Rose's mouth. I rolled my eyes. "Fine. I'll see you three later. Love you."

"We love you too," they called in one loud chorus.

I tried to not let their superstitious natures

distract me from driving home safely and getting ready. A few minutes, and he'd be at my house. I wasn't sure what we'd do, but I doubted being sticky and stinky would help any situation. I showered in record time, dressed in a simple pair of jeans and a flowery blouse, and was pleased I had extra time to apply mascara and lip gloss and even put on a small pair of silver hoop earrings.

The doorbell rang a few minutes after seven.

He was dressed in the same clothes and had a bright smile on his face. I invited him in and followed him to the small couch where we'd sat together the other day.

"How was dinner?" he asked.

Snowball trotted into the room, found his target, and jumped in Cam's lap.

I laughed and apologized, but Cam didn't seem to mind. In fact, he seemed almost thrilled to have the cat sit with him.

"Dinner was good. I went to the ninnies' house."

He scratched his head, looking thoroughly confused. "The ninnies?"

I smiled. Yep, it had been a good thing Cam hadn't gone with me. "Have you heard about the three identical sisters that live in the canyons. They're a little—"

"Crazy?"

I laughed. "That's what a lot of people think. But they're actually really sweet. They were my mom's best friends in high school, and when my parents died, they took me in as one of their own. I think you know Mary from the hospital. She's an anesthesiologist."

"Oh, Mary," he said recognition flashing through

his eyes. "Dark hair, bushy eyebrows?"

"Yep, that's the one."

"I like her. She's got spunk."

I nodded. "You should meet the other two. The three of them together are so much fun to be around."

"I'm glad someone was there to watch over you back then."

I nodded.

Cam shifted on the couch, bumping his knee against mine. "That's actually why I came, Well, one of the reasons."

I lifted an eyebrow. "You came to talk about the ninnies?"

He chuckled. "No. Yes. Kind of. I heard Millie's planning something. She has you working on a special project, doesn't she?"

"Uh…" How did he know?

"So I was right?"

I nodded. "She hired me to plan her wedding."

Cam huffed. "Who's she marrying?"

I shrugged. "I guess it's the guy she's been dating. I haven't even met him, but she's talked about him a lot."

"Well, I have to admit, that was pretty fast. Who's the guy?"

"His name is Phillip."

Cam stood up and started pacing the room. "That's impossible."

"What? Why? Do you know him?"

Cam took a few more seconds before lifting his head. "This is insane."

I widened my eyes. "What's insane? *You're* acting crazy. I thought you and Millie weren't together."

Cam's eyes darted around the house, then settled on me. "I'm Phillip. Phillip Camden. Only she calls me Phillip and always has. But I am most certainly not engaged to Millie."

My stomach twisted in knots as I repeated his words in my head. "So, she's not engaged?"

"Not unless there's another Phillip, but I doubt that." He sighed. "She's always doing this. Making stuff up in her head and imagining things will get better."

"Are you sure you broke things off? Because girls sometimes take a while to get the message."

He moved closer until our feet were toe-to-toe. "We're not together, even the tiniest bit. I need you to believe that."

I crossed my arms, waiting for an explanation. "Why would she dump a load of money into something that's not happening?"

He shrugged. "She dreams big." When I continued to look skeptical, he held up his hands. "You said you've never met Phillip; isn't that a little weird that you're planning his wedding and you've never met him? Do you have his measurements? Ordered his suit? Asked his preferences for the cake?"

"Well, no, but Millie has a lot of demands. I just figured her fiancé would be used to it."

Cam huffed. "There's no fiancé. Doesn't it seem a little weird you haven't even met the groom?"

"I'm only two days into planning. I still have twenty-five to go."

His face paled. "Twenty-five? Why twenty-five?"

I shrugged. "I don't know. It sounds crazy to me too. That's just what she said."

He hummed to himself. "What is she planning?"

I laughed. "A wedding, remember?"

Cam's eyes jerked to mine. "I can't make this any more clear. She's not marrying me or anybody else. She's delusional, and . . . I would never marry her."

I scooted closer and rubbed a hand across his back. "It's okay. I believe you."

He looked up with hope in his eyes. "You do?"

I looked around at my house. I'd just gotten it back, and it wasn't cheap either. I was barely making enough at the moment to have a little left over each month. If I refused to do my job now, I would lose everything. "Yes, but for my job's sake, I'm going to keep planning this wedding."

"You shouldn't be working for her at all."

I put my hands on my hips and pouted my lip out like a little girl. "You'll just have to be frustrated with the fact that I'm planning your fake wedding."

He chuckled wryly. "You're cute when you're being stubborn." He sighed and reached for my hand. I let him take it after a moment's hesitation. "I guess it won't matter either way, so go ahead and plan it."

I frowned at him. "You know, you're super cryptic sometimes."

He winked. "You'll get used to it."

I shrugged. As long as I got paid, I didn't really care. Actually, that wasn't entirely true, but it's what I told myself, since there was no other logical explanation for why I should care whom Millie married.

He let go of my hand and backed up next to the wall. "Okay, let's change the subject. I actually came over here for another, more important reason."

I tightened my arms around my chest. What could

he possibly have to say now?

Cam cleared his throat, his eyes growing more serious by the second. I waited for him to tell me something serious had happened, like he didn't want to see me anymore. Or he was dating someone else. Or even worse, that he was in the middle of a bad divorce. But what he said next was something I couldn't have guessed.

"I need someone to feed my fish."

I tilted my chin forward. "What?" I stared at him for a second before letting out a little laugh. "Why does everything you say seem so out-there?"

He chuckled and grabbed for the door. "Because it is. I've been too busy at work to come home, and I'm going to need someone to check on my fish. Will you come? Please?"

I shrugged. There were worse things a person could ask of you than feeding their fish. I should have expected some bizarre request from him by now. "Sure, I guess, though I am wondering how this is more important than us."

Chapter 15

He opened the door, letting a draft of cool, night air in. "I do love my fish. Now, do you mind driving?" he asked as I started the hunt for my keys.

I stood up and looked out the window at his truck, parked outside my house. Nothing seemed wrong with it. "You're a piece of work, you know that? So needy." I joked.

He smiled and wrapped an arm around my shoulder. "You're a lifesaver, you know that?"

Warmth spread down my back as he pulled me in closer. "I'll take you, but only if you help me find my keys."

He frowned, looking toward the couch where Snowball had sprawled himself across the two cushions. "Alright, kitty, time to find the keys."

A few minutes later, after finding the keys in the bathroom by the toilet, we were set to go. The drive to

Cam's house was more pleasant than I imagined it would be. A few seconds into the drive, he reached for my free hand, only letting go of it when I was turning a corner. We avoided topics that revolved around work, so that might have been why it was so pleasant. He led me back through the canyon and over by Avalanche Park.

I turned on the music, and as we chatted, we found we had similar tastes in music and books, but had opposite views on sports. He liked baseball, but I loved a good football game.

When we finally came to a lull in the conversation, I glanced over at him and smirked. "Okay, so what's the story? Why have you been neglecting your fish?"

He exhaled and focused his attention straight ahead. "The poor thing's probably starving. The hospital has kept me busy. Long hours, and I mostly sleep in the on-call rooms."

"You stay at the hospital?" I asked, trying to picture him brushing his teeth in some on-call room.

"Kind of. I've been tied up there, too tired to make it home. It's pretty regular for doctors to stick around a few days."

I had never heard of that, but I hadn't actually dated a doctor. I stilled. Were we dating? We hadn't kissed, but we'd held hands and cuddled some. *I don't want to think about this right now.* "Tell me about your fish."

He nodded. "Swordy is a Yellow Tang with a pointy nose in the shape of a sword. He's got a fun personality. If you tap on the bowl, he'll beat his head against the glass. Don't do it too much, or else he'll get

138

a red bump on his forehead."

I laughed, seeing guilt cross his face. He must've experimented doing this one too many times. "That's cute. So do you think you'll go home tonight, you know, after I drive you back to my house?"

Cam looked out the window, and I saw a sadness sweep over him. "I don't think so. The hospital is going through . . . some changes right now, and it's impossible to leave."

I nodded, understanding how someone could get lost in work responsibilities. "Well, I can't wait to meet Swordy. And I wouldn't mind going back and feeding him every day if you needed me to. You live really close to where I work."

His face lit up. "That would be awesome. The key is in a flower pot by the door, buried in the bottom, so if you ever needed to stay, it would be fine with me."

While he typed the address into my phone, I thought of what else he might need. "Do you want me to bring you anything else? Clothes? Food? Check the mail? Anything like that?"

He shook his head, thinking for a minute. "No, I'm pretty hooked up there. Maria takes care of the mail, and Joe and Jasmine have brought me clothes. I've set up in one of the older rooms, sleeping on one of the beds. It's a little musty, but more private than the other rooms. Just kind of quiet."

I smiled, glad he didn't seem too distressed by work. Eventually, we came back around to talking about Millie's fake wedding. He asked about the wedding plans and stared quietly out the window as he listened to every response. I told him about the flowers she wanted, the dress she had picked out and wanted special-ordered at whatever cost, and even the lack of information about Phillip. Whenever I thought he was bored with the topic, I would end my answer and move to turn up the music. But then he'd ask another wedding-planning question.

By the time we reached his neighborhood, my throat was dry from talking so much. Each house here was big enough to swallow mine and then some. I pulled up to his, the most modest on the street, though not that much smaller than its fellows. It was beautiful with its navy-blue siding on the top half of the house and beige stone as its foundation.

"This is your house?" I asked, wondering what he must've thought of my tiny home. I probably couldn't even afford the land for his driveway.

He nodded but didn't say any more.

"For some reason, I pictured you in this big apartment penthouse with a man cave and everything."

He laughed heartily, sending a tingle of pleasure down my spine. I loved to make this man laugh.

He stayed back near the steps as we approached the porch. "Better check to make sure the key is still there. Only Joe and Jasmine know about it."

I walked up the front porch steps and dug my hand into the gardenia flower pot. It took a while, but finally, I fished out a thick, silver key. "Still here."

Then I unlocked the door. "Home sweet home," Cam said, slipping in behind me. I shut the door, then whirled around for my first glance. My mouth dropped open. It was perfect.

"Be right back," he said. "I've got to check on a few things. Take a self-guided tour, and I'll meet you upstairs. My room is all the way in the back."

I nodded and then waited a few seconds before taking a deep whiff of his house. His smell surrounded me. Ooh, I loved it. Leather, cologne, and almonds.

My eyes moved across the house, from the kitchen and dining area in front of me to the sitting room to my right. There was a long, wide hallway to my left that led to a full staircase. The house was full of modern furnishings, and everything looked new and very breakable. The sitting room had a variety of couches that led to an open kitchen with bar stools around a long island.

I continued my tour upstairs, checking out the bedrooms, each filled with either a bed, an office, or a hobby. I laughed when I saw his collection of Avengers memorabilia.

Finally, I found his room tucked at the back of the upstairs hallway. It was enormous, with a king-sized bed, a jetted tub in the bathroom, and a door that led to a balcony. It was open, so I made my way outside. I couldn't help sighing when I walked onto the balcony to see the stars shining above me.

"Great view, huh?" he said, coming up behind me. I jumped, nearly slamming into the railing. He had been perched along the back wall while he waited for me.

He chuckled and moved up next to me. "Sorry, I didn't think you'd jump that much."

I laughed off my embarrassment. "Your house is amazing. Like really? I see the appeal in these big houses. Still, you must have spent a fortune."

Cam leaned forward, resting his arms across the railing. "Yeah, it's nice when you can pay for your schooling as you go."

"You don't have any student loans?"

"Nope. My grandfather made sure all of us grandchildren had a nice college fund to rely on. But just so we're clear, having a big house with no one to fill it seems pointless. I'm rarely home."

A pang of sympathy struck my heart, and I stepped forward and squeezed his arm softly. He looked up at the stars and away from my face. Even though I should've looked away, I couldn't. He looked so handsome in the moonlight. After a minute, he turned and leaned against the railing, facing me.

I shivered and wrapped my arms around myself, not knowing if the shivering was because of the cold or his intense stare.

He tentatively moved closer. "You're cold."

My teeth started to chatter. We'd left in a hurry, and I had grabbed the jacket nearest the door, a light windbreaker. "Well, I wasn't until you reminded me."

He chuckled and moved forward to pull me toward him. He reached for me and then asked, "May I?"

My heart thumped loudly inside my chest as I nodded, and he pulled me in. His smell, his touch, it was all too much. I shivered again, but this time from pure bliss.

He chuckled as he wrapped his arms around me. He didn't have a jacket on, and, though his skin felt as cold as mine, there was no way I was pulling out of his embrace. For the first time all night, I relaxed. I leaned my head against his shoulder while he rested his chin against my cheek. Oh man, what had I been missing out on? There was no going back from this kind of feeling. A fizzing energy filled me from head to toe, and when he shifted, it bubbled up all over again.

I peeked up at him. He was looking at me, a smile tickling the edges of his mouth. "Have I ever told you how amazing I think you are?"

The air whooshed out of me, and all I could squeeze out was a weak-voiced, "Me?"

"Yes, you." He took one of my hands and squeezed it. "I tried to fight this feeling inside, thinking it was too soon to feel this way, but I can't anymore. Which is why I want Millie far away from you."

My smile slipped from my face.

He sighed. "I need to stop bringing her up, huh?"

I nodded, biting my lip.

The more he talked about her, the more I doubted that he was over Millie. Finally I said, "This makes no sense to me either, but I feel this tie to you."

He moved a piece of hair out of my eyes, sending a shiver down my face and neck.

Then he pulled me back in and hugged me closer. "Before I say something stupid, I think we should go meet my fish. Especially since I am relying on you to take care of my only family member."

I laughed. "Okay." I dropped my arms with some reluctance, but almost immediately he reached for one of my hands and held it tightly.

On our way inside, Cam pointed to the glass bowl on his nightstand.

"May I?" I asked.

He nodded, and I rushed over to see a little yellow fish with a sword-shaped lump on his nose. "He looks pretty good so maybe my housekeeper has been feeding him enough."

He has a housekeeper? I swallowed down that information, trying not to react. "There you are, Swordy," I said cooing and tapping the glass. Swordy swam headfirst into the glass, a little thump vibrating the water. I smiled and looked around for some fish food. A little green bottle of food was hidden behind a lampshade, and when I started opening it, Swordy swam to the surface and started splashing around.

"All right, here it is buddy." I dropped in a few flakes and sat on the edge of Cam's bed to watch. He sat next to me, rubbing a thumb over the back of my hand.

"Thank you for coming here," he said. "And being with me."

"Anytime." I stared up into his beautiful eyes, warmth filling my cheeks. There was no denying how I felt now. I definitely had feelings for Cam.

He moved closer, making my heart rattle around like a rocket inside my chest. He was going to kiss me. *Finally.* I stilled, not wanting to spook him, but not knowing if I was even ready for this step in our relationship. As his face got closer to mine, I closed my eyes and waited. And waited. And then opened them again because I felt ridiculous.

He had backed up a few inches and was staring at me, a small smile on his face. My heart raced as he scrutinized my face with his eyes.

"We better get going," he said, standing up and going toward the door.

Disappointment and rejection flooded my entire body, but I had no other choice than to follow him. Why didn't he want to kiss me, and what was I getting myself into . . . falling for a guy I barely knew?

Chapter 16

Four days went by and after that night, I fell into a pattern—planning a possibly fake wedding, doing my best to avoid Millie's moods, going to the gym every other day, and running into Cam on my way home from the hospital each night. Twice, we talked by my car in the parking lot, but whenever I asked him if he wanted to go somewhere, he claimed to be busy and always kept a wide berth from my lips. At least he still held my hand.

Toward the end of the work week, it was time to report to Millie on my progress. Before the meeting, I went to my office to grab her folder. Cam was standing in my office's doorway, blocking my way.

"What are you doing here?" I hissed, shooing him backwards into my office. I looked around for lingering eyes, especially Millie's, and then shut the door behind me. "You better hope Millie's in her office. If she saw you were here for me, she'd flip."

Cam shook his head, a sly smile on his face. "She's in her office."

"You saw her?" I said, worry building in my chest. Had they been talking? Meeting?

He moved closer to me. "Yes, but only for a second. Don't worry. It's like I wasn't even here."

I doubted that. Anxiety rose in my chest. What kind of mood would she be in because of that visit?

I pressed myself against the door and kept my hands tightly at my side. I didn't want a repeat of the other night at his house, no matter how much I wanted him to reach out and hold me. "So, what are you doing here?"

He sighed. "Have you found Joe's number yet?"

I lifted an eyebrow. "Oh man, I forgot. I've just been so—"

"Please, please, find it and call him." He puffed up his cheeks, then sighed. "Before I say anything, I need you to talk to him."

I crossed my arms protectively in front of me, guarding myself from showing any emotion. "You're worrying me. Don't you think Jasmine would have called me back if it was this important? Maybe she doesn't want to talk about it."

He ran a hand through his hair. "I know it sounds crazy, but just call them."

Brittney's voice echoed down the hall, sending fear crawling up my spine. What if she found me with Cam? Brittney was not good at keeping secrets, and I did not need another thing to worry about.

I held a finger to his soft lips. "It's the girl I work with," I whispered. "If she sees me with you, it might get back to Millie. You have to go."

He wrapped an arm around me. "I just want you to know I'm still really interested in you. There are just some things I am not in control of right now, and Jaz will be the better one to tell you."

"Okay, I promise. I will not leave this resort today until I talk to one of them."

He smiled, the movement of his lips sending a tingle down my arm. "Will you meet me in the hospital parking lot—where you always park—tonight, after you talk to them?"

I put my back to the door and discreetly locked it, just in case Brittney came bounding in. Just in time too. The door jiggled and then a knock came. "Rory, are you in here? Millie wants us."

I took a deep breath and tried to answer calmly. "Yep, just shutting down. Meet you up there in a few minutes."

"Okay, but hurry up. I heard there's a sale at the beauty shop in town."

I rolled my eyes and listened as her steps grew quieter. Then I sighed and turned to see Cam studying me.

He grimaced. "Until tonight." He stepped closer so his lips were inches from mine.

My heart sped up, and I counted the beats as they pounded in my head.

"You're cute when you blush." He lifted his hand to my cheek. In comparison to his cold hands, my face felt on fire.

I bit my lip. "You need to go or you might ruin everything."

He leaned in to whisper in my ear. "So I'll see you

tonight?"

I shivered as his lips brushed past my ear. I stole a glance into his eyes and felt my knees weakening. "Either that or I'm sleeping in my office as I try to call Jasmine."

He chuckled quietly. "I believe you. Just wait in the parking lot around 8:00, and I'll be there. If it takes me a minute, don't go anywhere."

I unlocked the door and checked the hallway, but Brittney was gone. "Go." I put a hand on his back and pushed him out. My fingers tingled against his thin shirt. Where was his jacket? He walked toward the stairway and didn't look back.

I went back into the office to catch my breath and gather my tablet, then counted to thirty and headed up the stairs. Cam was long gone by the time I made it into the stairwell, and I practically ran up to Millie's office.

Brittney was waiting outside her door. She crossed her arms and narrowed her gaze at me. "What is going on? These last few days, you've been skipping around this place."

I shrugged. "Just another day."

She shook her head, her normal red lips more shocking than her usual outrageously-colored lipstick. "Don't give me that. We are not going into Millie's office until you tell me. What's going on?"

"Not here," I said, moving her to the closest bathroom, down the hall. We went inside and I checked that the stalls were empty.

Brittney crossed her arms and stood in front of the door to block it. "See, what is this? You're acting all secretive."

I sighed and moved toward a sink. I patted some water on my cheeks and forehead and turned to her, needing to cool down for a lot of reasons. "I met someone." My voice came out small and worried. I wouldn't tell her it was Cam, but there was still a risk in telling her anything.

Brittney's face lit up. "What's wrong with that? You don't look happy about it."

I sighed. "Do you remember when I got a signature from that instructor at the hospital?"

Brittney nodded. "Yes, just another way that woman abuses your very capable skills."

I nodded. "Well, the doctor taking care of the guy was, well, we had a connection."

When her face started to light up again, I stopped her. "He told me he wasn't interested in seeing anyone. But we've kind of been hanging out anyway. Then last week we . . . almost kissed."

Brittney gasped and covered her mouth with mock exaggeration. "You didn't! You almost kissed him?"

I pushed her away playfully. "There's more. This guy used to be Millie's fiancé."

Brittney's mouth dropped open. "Wait, hold the phone. You're dating Phillip Camden?!"

I sighed. "See, how did you even know about him?"

Brittney looked sideways at me. "How did you *not* know? He's all over her desk; he used to stop by all the time. He even owns half of the resort."

I widened my eyes. "How do you know all this?"

"Girl, I listen, and I'm not so busy working that I don't have time to gossip too. Maybe you should work

149

a little less too, because then you wouldn't be dating someone else's fiancé."

I shook my head, a small smile growing on my face. "They're not engaged."

"What? How could they not—"

"He said she made it all up. They broke up months ago."

Brittney rubbed her hands together. "Oh man, the plot just thickened. You gotta tell Millie you know."

"And get fired? Yeah right."

"No, call her on it. He's your man now, right?"

"Well, technically, I guess."

"Then stake your claim, girl."

The bathroom door slammed open, pushing Brittney into me. It was the only person that could make me want to disappear on the spot.

Millie.

"Um, what are you girls doing? We have a meeting scheduled for five minutes ago. Move your feet or lose your jobs."

We followed silently behind her, though Brittney's face was speaking volumes. But I couldn't just "call Millie on it". Maybe I didn't have to tell her *I* was with him, but just that I knew he was dating someone else.

Millie pointed to the two chairs and then sat across from us. "Ok, girls, report."

Brittney went first, reviewing the event with the Phishler company, talking about the three bookings she'd secured, and the status of the two leadership conferences that were scheduled for next week.

All that time, I continued to review the words of my speech in my head, but as soon as Millie's attention whipped to me, my mouth turned to cotton.

"Well, spit it out. What have you wasted your time with this week?"

I cleared my throat and swallowed down the dryness. "Yes, okay. The flowers, the food, and your dress have been ordered, exactly as you wanted." That had been the good part. Time to speed up. "We are renting linens from Diamond Rental, though they didn't have gold linens in stock. So, I chose your second choice—crème."

"What, what? Did you call Linens Exported? How about Crown Rental?"

I nodded my head at each suggestion. "Sixteen days is not much time to give people notice."

Millie eyes narrowed to slits. "That's enough time, Rory. Maybe you're just too incompetent to handle this responsibility."

I clenched my jaw and remembered the pep talk Brittney had given me. "If you don't like it, you can make the calls yourself. Then you'll see how truly impossible this event is."

Millie's glare turned to Brittney. "Brittney, can you do better?"

Brittney ran a hand over her lip, as if she knew there wasn't enough color there. "Nope, I don't think so. You can't get better than Rory. I've seen her this whole week, whittling companies down to their best deals, begging for extra time limits, more accommodations—"

"Okay, I get it," Millie said, holding her hands up in defeat. "Well, if that's the case, this is the week we move our focus to Phillip."

Brittney gave me a pointed look. "Do something,"

she whispered.

Millie ignored her if she heard, plowing ahead. "Here is a new folder with all things you need for him. I had him sized, with some difficulty, and everything should be good to go."

She slid a folder over to me. I opened it quickly and reviewed its contents. Pretty typical. Not a lot of explanation, too many numbers, and not a single picture to go off of. I just needed to confirm that Phillip was actually Cam. There was still an itty-bitty chance that she had met a new Phillip and was dating someone else.

"So, do you have a picture of him? I need to see him. Measurements are not enough. I need to see his skin color, his hair color, his eye color."

Millie's smile wavered. "Well, you can't really meet him. He's much too occupied. But here's a picture. Honestly, I'm surprised you didn't make a connection earlier since you've already met him."

She grabbed a photo from the desk, one I'd always seen the back side of, though never the front. So, Phillip's picture *had* been on her desk all along. Then spun it around. My heart dropped to my feet.

I was staring into the beautiful eyes of the man I knew as Cam.

Chapter 17

Indignation started to build in my chest, and I knew I couldn't keep quiet. "This is Cam," I said matter-of-factly, my voice stiff but strong.

"Cam? No, this is Phillip. Only his pesky friends call him by his last name. His real name is Phillip Camden."

My hands shook as I reached forward and held the picture. There was no doubt now. Out of Millie's line of sight, Brittney patted my leg.

"But you can't be with him," I said, stumbling over my words. I bit my tongue and lied. "I heard he's dating someone new."

Her face soured. "Look at the picture if you don't believe me."

I looked at the time stamp. The picture had been taken almost a year ago. "That was a long time ago. He's with someone else now. Why have we been planning a fake wedding?"

Millie stood up, challenging me with her scary eyes. "Excuse me?"

Anger started to build in my chest, the adrenaline giving me courage. "Yeah, I know your secret. You and Cam are not really together."

Millie slammed her fist on the desk, making Brittney and I jump. "I've paid my dues to that man, and we are getting married. I've been with him almost every night, and, when he finally wakes up, he will know I stood by his side."

"What?" *What did that even mean?*

Her angry expression melted into a pleased smile. "Oh, you don't know? I thought you knew everything about "Cam," she said, holding up air quotes with her fingers. "When's the last time you saw him, huh?"

"Yesterday," I lied. There was no way I'd tell her about the private meeting we'd just had in my office.

"That's impossible," she said, practically spitting at me. "I saw him last night, and he was in the same condition."

My stomach cramped together tightly. What was she talking about? "What condition? What are you talking about? He's fine."

Millie's face went from weary to menacing, and she clenched her teeth together as she talked. "I don't have time to talk about this anymore. You obviously have no idea what you're talking about. Go to the hospital and find him yourself if you don't believe me. I have nothing to prove to you. In the meantime, you will never question me again, Rory. This wedding is happening and you are planning it. Now, get! Out! You too, Brittney."

154

The two of us stood quickly and scrambled to get out of her office. Before I could leave, she called for me once more.

"Don't forget this," she snapped. Millie edged the folder toward the edge of the desk.

I stared at it, then snatched the manila folder off her desk in one swipe, but not before she caught my wrist. "I'm on to you, Rory. If you do anything to mess up this wedding, I will sue you for every penny that you have. I will destroy your name and any career chances you could ever have. Do you understand?"

I clamped my mouth shut, swallowing hard. I nodded, then ran out of the office. My hands shook as I closed Millie's door behind me.

Brittney stood by the door, a smug look on her face. "You did it," she said, whispering until we were far enough away that Millie couldn't possibly overhear. My feet felt like bricks as we continued down the hall. "You stood up to that old witch."

"Yeah, and now, she's threatened to destroy me. I don't understand. She makes it seem like he's been in an accident or something, but I swear I just saw him."

Brittney raised her eyebrows. "Well, I guess there's only one way for you to know the truth. Go find him.'"

Chapter 18

After Brittney left for the day, I locked the office and got on the phone to call the only person I knew who could give me Joe's information.

"This is Mrs. Jessie. What can I do for you?"

I breathed a sigh of relief. "Mrs. Jessie, I need your help. You have numbers to all the employees at the resort, right? Even the ski instructors?"

"Yes, I think so. Do you need something?"

"Yes. Remember the guy who got in the accident a few weeks ago? Joe?"

"Yeah, sweet guy. Haven't seen him around much."

I sighed, crossing my fingers. "I really need his number."

"Okay, well, give me a minute to track it down."

I smiled, loving Mrs. Jessie even more. Why hadn't I tried this before? In three minutes, she had tracked down the number. I thanked her, hung up my office phone, and picked up my cell. I twirled a pen in one hand as I punched in the numbers.

It rang twice before Joe answered.

"Hello?" His voice was not the cheerful one I had expected. Instead, he sounded beaten.

"Joe, hey, this is Rory. I've been trying to get ahold of you two for a while. How are you doing?"

Joe was quiet for a second, and I checked to make sure I hadn't hung up on him. "Hey, Rory."

"Whoa, Joe, you don't sound so good. I was just wondering if Jasmine's been getting my messages?"

He paused and then said, "Yeah, yeah. She's been struggling too. We've both taken the news really hard."

An ice-cold foreboding crawled up my spine. Did this have anything to do with what Millie had said? "News? What news? What's wrong? Has something happened to Cam?"

Joe made a noise that sounded like sobbing. "You . . . you haven't heard?"

My throat tightened, and I struggled to speak past the paralyzing chill. "No. Heard what?"

"Cam was in a car accident."

I dropped the pen I'd been twirling. "What?" I grabbed my purse and keys and practically ran across my tiny office.

"After our ski date, Cam's truck slipped off the side of the canyon and fell into a ravine."

I stopped moving, the keys frozen at the lock in the door. "But how? I've—" I clamped my mouth shut. Joe was a nice person, but I wasn't sure I should tell him about seeing Cam, a bizarre event in light of this news. "So, he's in the hospital? Right now?" I finally asked, my words coming out too thickly.

"Yeah, he is. Look, Rory, I have to go, but I'm sorry we didn't call you sooner. We thought you would know by now. I'm sure he'd love a visit from you."

"Thanks, Joe. I'll go check on him."

Not only had Millie told me it was impossible to have seen Cam, now Joe had confirmed it.

So what had I been seeing? A ghost?

But that was crazy. There was a logical explanation for everything. There had to be.

I hurried to my car, rushing past the Jessies, whose looks of concern would have been enough to stop me in my tracks if the injured person had been anyone other than Cam.

Only after I was safely locked in my car did I let my calm façade fade away. I dropped my arms to the steering wheel and collapsed against it, shaking.

After a full minute of taking deep breaths, I started the car. I had to know right now what was going on. I was supposed to meet Cam at the hospital in a few minutes anyway. There was still a chance this was all a cruel joke. Everything would be fine once I saw him.

I drove to the hospital, faster and more recklessly than ever. The whole drive over, Millie's words rang in my head like a bell.

The sky was dark as I pulled into the hospital. When I parked in my usual spot, furthest away from the hospital, he stood there at the streetlight smiling, looking as handsome as ever in a sweater and khaki pants as he waited for me.

Relief washed over me. I wasn't crazy. He was

158

right there. His smile disappeared as I stormed out of the car and came running to him.

"You're here," I said, breathing fast. I reached out to touch him, and he was as solid as he ever had been. I hugged him close, burying my face in his chest. He held me closer, pressing his lips to my hair.

"I'm here," he said, though there was a question in his voice. He held onto my arms and pushed back so he could see my face. "You talked to Joe, didn't you?"

My words caught in my throat, and I cried against him. "I don't understand. You're right here. At first, I thought Millie was crazy when she said she had stayed by your side every night, and then I thought it was impossible that I'd seen you yesterday. But I did, didn't I?"

He tucked a piece of hair behind my ear. "Yes, you did. It's okay. Tell me what happened next."

I sighed, though the tight knot in my chest remained in place. "But then Joe said you were in a car accident. The night of our date. He said you're in the hospital right now." My eyes raked over him as I searched for bruises or cuts or anything that told me he wasn't okay. "You don't look like you've been in an accident. You must be better if they let you out every once in a while. Right? I'm not crazy. You're here. I'm not crazy."

Cam's face went slack, and the color seemed to drain away. He reached out and tapped my chin with his finger, lifting it so lightly I could barely feel him. "Do you trust me?"

We'd been through some weird moments together in the last few weeks, but I had no reason not to trust him. I nodded. "I trust you."

He sighed. "I've been trying to think of a way to tell you this. It's strange, out-of-this-world strange, but I need you to trust me before I drop this bomb."

I released his hand. "Okay, now you're really scaring me."

Someone tapped my shoulder, and I spun to the side. A man dressed in black with a hoodie covering his head towered over me. "What are you doing out here all alone, girly?" His voice was gravelly and dark.

I stepped back toward Cam, goosebumps traveling down my arms and legs. "We were just talking."

The guy glanced around, then back at me. "*We?* Well, *we* can make things interesting."

Cam whispered in my ear. "Go toward the hospital, Rory. Run."

My legs refused to move. Would this guy really attack me in front of Cam? "Cam, it's fine. You're here—"

"Who are you talking to, sweetie?" He moved closer. I moved backward, pulling Cam with me.

Cam met my eyes, panic crossing his face. "No, I'm not. I'm not here. Go, Rory. Run!"

"W-what?"

His face was deeply worried now, and he was paler than ever. "Go to the hospital and tell them you're my sister. Go! Go now!"

"Where're you going? Party just started." The guy's breath stank of booze.

Cam was shoving me away from the car. "You need to run, Rory. This guy wants to hurt you, and I am not here to protect you. Run! Now!"

Then Cam disappeared.

160

Chapter 19

I turned on my heel, but Cam was gone. Spinning a full circle, I didn't see him anywhere. He was gone. "Cam? Where'd you go?" My voice was tight and scared as I backed up toward the hospital, away from the man.

The man was getting closer, his intentions deep in the black pit of his eyes. Adrenaline shot through me, and I ran. I ran toward the hospital and didn't look back. I could hear him huffing hard behind me, but the sounds grew quieter, and by the time I reached the hospital doors, I risked a glance back. The man had stopped in the parking lot.

"Your loss, baby," he called to me.

I spun around and ran right for the front desk. A white-haired lady sat behind the receptionist desk, her eyes growing wider as I made a beeline for her.

"Help," I said, my voice a little hoarse. "There's a

guy in the parking lot harassing me."

She stood up, her eyes growing softer with every second. "Oh, sweetheart. Come over here and sit down. My name's Joyce. You look like you've seen a ghost."

Maybe I have.

She led me to a chair and motioned for a security guard to join us. They listened while I breathlessly related the incident with the harasser. After I'd had a minute to calm down, I remembered Cam.

I turned to Joyce. "Please, I need to see Cam. Dr. Camden."

My words came out breathy and tired. Joyce looked sympathetic as she shook her head. "Honey, Dr. Camden isn't available right now. Since his accident, no one's allowed to see him unless they are family."

My heart dropped to my stomach. So he was in the hospital right now? Fear crawled up my spine. Doubt and suspicion took turns battling inside my mind. My voice shook as I answered. "Uh . . . right."

I remembered what Cam said right before he disappeared. *He disappeared!* I took a deep breath and tried to keep myself together. "I'm his sister and just wanted to check on him."

"Oh, you're his sister. Poor dear," she said patting my arm. "You've already been through enough, and now you've got people harassing you in the parking lot. Well, I will take care of that. You focus on Dr. Camden. What's your name so I know you're on his list."

Panic struck me. "Jasmine," I said quickly.

"Oh, there you are right there."

I sighed in relief.

"Right now he's in room 345 on the third floor."

After another minute of assuring her everything was fine, I scrambled to the elevator, punching the third-floor button as fast as I could. Was this what Cam had meant to tell me? Well, of course I wouldn't have believed him.

My head spun with dizziness. This couldn't be happening. Cam couldn't be with me only minutes before and now stuck in the hospital. I picked at my lip as the elevator climbed two flights and then dinged open. I straightened my blouse and prepared for the worst. If something was wrong, I didn't want to make things worse.

The room numbers grew higher as I walked down the hall. 340, 342, 344.

I gasped when I reached the right door. Acid churned in my stomach as I entered, and I gasped as I recognized the man in bed. Though he looked much smaller under a layer of wires and hookups, there was no doubt it was Cam. The impossibility of him being in here so weak and vulnerable and not having just left me was too much to take in.

I spun around and ran for the elevator. My heart thumped hard in my chest, and I held a hand to my mouth to keep from sobbing. Before I could make it to the privacy of an elevator, someone stopped me with their hand.

I looked up into the kind eyes of Mary.

"You just found out, didn't you?" she asked softly.

"Mary. Oh, Mary. I don't understand what's happening." She took me into her arms right as the tears started.

"Come with me, Sweetie." She took my hand and led me past the front room, down the hall, and into a tiny exam room where she helped me to a seat.

Mary shut the door, then sat down in a chair next to me. "Okay, start at the beginning."

"You wouldn't believe me if I told you," I said, half-laughing, half-crying.

"Try me," she said, her voice patient.

I nodded and took a deep breath before speaking. "Cam and I have been seeing each other the last few weeks. We see each other almost every day, though it's mostly been at the hospital. And just now, he was in the parking lot—" My voice broke, and Mary reached for my hand.

"Yes, I'm with you so far. Keep going."

I cleared my throat, trying to swallow down the hard knot building there. "And then we were just in the parking lot outside, and this guy shows up." I stopped talking to catch my breath. Mary waited patiently, rubbing my back and giving me time to think.

"The creeper started coming toward us, but then . . . Cam just disappears . . . in the middle of nowhere. Just like that, he was gone. And then I ran from the guy. And then the receptionist said . . . and I came up here. And he's in the bed. He's been here all along." I put my head in my hands and sobbed. "I don't understand what's happening. Was it all real or in my head? Is something wrong with me?"

Mary lifted my chin with her finger and smiled softly at me. "Nothing is wrong with you. I totally believe that he could have come to you—out of body. Crazier things have happened. But he's been here in a

164

coma for over two weeks."

I stopped moving, stopped breathing. "So he *was* in a car accident?" I said, wanting to make sure I had heard her right.

Mary checked her watch and nodded. "Remember the night of the big snow storm, that weekend you came and ate with us?"

"Yeah, that was the night of our first date, and it was snowing a lot. The hospital needed him for an emergency shift. He was supposed to call me when he was there safe, but I didn't hear from him until after I left your house. He just showed up at the house."

Mary raised an eyebrow. "Well, let's back up. On the night of the snowstorm, he was on his way to the hospital, but he never made it. He must've gone back home and was coming through the canyon. His truck slid and fell, crashing in the ravine below."

My heart dropped to my stomach as my parents' accident flashed through my mind. "He never . . ." I held a finger to my forehead, my mind spinning with this news. "So, he's been here . . . all this time?"

"Yes. He's been in a coma since they found him in a ravine. It's a miracle he didn't die."

I clasped my hand over my mouth and cried. "He almost died? But how? I've seen him. We've talked and run together. He told me where his house key was, and we've fed Swordy together. He's held my hand."

She nodded. "Strange, indeed, but not impossible. Cam hasn't responded much since the accident. I've taken a special interest in him, checking on him during my breaks."

"Well, that would explain why he never called or

texted me back."

Mary nodded. "Millie's been itching to get her hands on his phone, but the hospital is holding all of his belongings."

"But you knew this whole time? Why didn't you tell me?"

She squeezed my hand. "I wanted to, but things were supposed to unfold in their own time. He's been visiting you, right?"

I nodded, though I couldn't be sure. Had I been dreaming every time? No, we'd been in public; well, mostly. He had turned down going to the ninnies. And that time the nurses had walked right through him on the way to the gym for the first time. Had they literally walked right through him?

Mary patted my hand and gave me a sad smile. "Then it probably wouldn't have gone over well to tell you he's been in a coma the whole time. It might have messed up things that you did experience with him. And then there are rules about keeping things confidential about patients. I couldn't tell you, even if I wanted to."

"So you've been checking on him?"

She nodded. "Usually in the late evenings. It's the only time Millie will leave him alone. She hates it when I come."

I shook my head. "I'm pretty sure she'd hate anyone coming. You know, I've been planning their wedding."

"Cam's engaged to her?"

"Well, he said he wasn't, but then again, I guess I can't take the word of a ghost." I laughed at how ludicrous it all sounded, and the knot in my chest released a little. "I think I'm going crazy. Like literally, something is wrong with me. I have invented an entire relationship in my head."

A sudden desire to see him and to hold his real hand hit me with so much force that I stood and ran for the door. "I have to see him. Now! I have to see him now."

She checked her watch. "I'm sure Millie is here by now. She comes around this time every night, stays for an hour or so, and talks on her phone the whole visit."

"Can you get her to leave so I can visit him?"

She stood, and a wide grin stretched across her face. "With pleasure. I'll tell her I'm bathing him. She never likes to stick around for that. Give me five minutes, and the room is all yours." Suddenly, her eyebrows lowered, and I could tell she was battling whether to tell me something.

"What is it?" I asked.

"I do have a little more bad news."

I swallowed hard, not knowing if I could take any more. "Okay, what is it?"

"Since Cam is a doctor, he has all of his medical forms filled out."

I nodded, not sure where this was going.

"A long time ago, Cam signed an end-of-life agreement. After a certain amount of time, if he was still on life support or in a coma, Cam asked to be released from all care."

Tears came to my eyes. "When is his time up?" I squeaked out.

"In thirteen days."

Chapter 20

As Mary left the room, my mind went into panic mode. What if Cam woke up and saw me standing there? It's not like we had known each other long before his accident. Would he even remember our time together before the accident? During his coma? Had he been dreaming when he came to me?

And even worse, what if he didn't wake up and I never saw him again? There were so many new questions that scared me. The minutes passed quickly as I thought of all the possibilities, and, when Mary opened the door, I wasn't ready.

"It's all clear. I love telling annoying people to go away." She gave me a gentle smile and pulled me in for a hug. "Everything will be fine."

I nodded and headed in the direction of Cam's room. Instead of following me, Mary stayed at the door. "Aren't you coming too?" I asked.

She gestured for me to go ahead without her. "I'll make sure no one interrupts your visit. Take your time."

It seemed like a long walk the second time down the hall. The air was chillier, the walls a little too white. The door was closed when I approached it. I closed my eyes and took a deep breath.

Then I opened the door.

The room was quiet except for the machines. They made tiny hissing sounds as they assisted Cam's chest to rise and fall with each click. His body looked so frail, the white sheets a perfect match for his pale complexion.

Taking a tentative step toward the bed, I watched his face. He remained motionless, though his eyes moved behind closed lids. His hands were by his side outside of the thin sheet lying atop him. He was dressed in a hospital gown, his face freshly shaven. At least he was being well taken care of here. Or maybe Millie had done that.

I sighed. *Millie.* They must still be together. Or were they?

His hands rested at his side, and I couldn't help myself. I reached for his left hand. It was warm and not lifeless, like I had been expecting. There was no ring, but that didn't mean anything. Most guys didn't wear an engagement ring.

Instead of letting his hand go, I curled my fingers around his. I sat on the edge of the bed, keeping his hand in both of mine, searching for the right words to say.

"I don't know where to start," I said, my voice

169

cracking.

"Try by saying 'Hi'."

Cam's voice sounded behind me. I turned and saw him standing by the door. My legs shook as I stood. I looked down at my hand, still holding his, then back to the ghost version of Cam. I laid his hand back on the bed and stepped away. "You're here! What are you— How did you—"

He nodded. "You've got questions for me, I'm sure. But do me a favor and take my hand again?" I stepped forward, but he shook his head. "My real hand. It's the first time mine have felt warm in ages."

Cam dropped his hands, and I sat back on the bed and took Cam's real hand. Ghost-Cam came around the side of the bed and flexed his fingers and grinned. "Feels amazing after being empty for so long."

My pulse raced inside me as I looked between the two Cams. This was too surreal. "Maybe I have a brain tumor. Maybe that's why you're appearing to me."

Ghost-Cam chuckled and lifted up his hand. "Here, follow my finger with your eyes."

He moved his index finger back and forth in front of my face, and I obediently followed its direction. After a minute, he dropped his hand. "You don't have a brain tumor. This is just one of those weird . . . occurrences. Let's just call it a blessing right now. You're the only one who knows, and I need your help."

I squeezed his hand, hoping he felt that too. "You have some explaining to do, and since I don't know where to start, tell me everything."

He nodded. "I can do that now. I'm just glad you're here. One minute I was with you and that imbecile and next, I'm back in here, trapped from leaving. Are you okay?"

I looked at him in shock, my eyes filling with tears. "Am *I* okay?" I turned to gesture to his comatose body. "How could you even ask about me? I'm fine. I'm alive. Are *you* okay?"

He came over to me and held me close. I found his hand and wrapped it about my waist. "Mary said you got in an accident coming home from my house. I knew something was wrong when you didn't call me."

He shrugged. "Instincts are usually right. When I left your house, I realized I'd forgotten my travel bag. I made a few calls, then headed back into the storm. The roads were bad, much worse than before. I had a few scary calls, but I was almost out of the canyon, so I didn't want to stop. On the edge of the canyon, right where that little waterfall is, my truck slipped on some ice and fell in the ravine."

My hands shook in my lap. Just like what had happened with my parents. Same canyon. Same dangerous driving conditions. I sobbed as I thought of the comparison. "You could have died. Mary said it was a miracle someone even noticed you and called 911."

Cam gestured to his motionless body on the bed. "I don't look very alive, do I? I kind of just floated away from my body after it happened. Kind of cool, really."

"Don't joke," I said, tears falling faster now.

He frowned. "I've tried everything to return. I've tried to jump back in my body, fitting it perfectly. I tried to contact other people, but you seem to be the only one who can hear and touch me. My time is almost up, and I need your help."

171

I looked at him in what I knew could only be desperation. "But how can I help? Mary said you've already signed some papers."

He sighed. "I would've never signed them if I'd known. I have thirteen days for you to figure out a way to save me and give me more time."

I gulped and wiped at my face. "Tall order. Why didn't you tell me?"

He sighed and buried his face in his hands. "And put your job in even more risk? Millie's been here every day, guarding me. If she saw you—if she knew—I didn't want to put your job in more jeopardy than it already seems to be."

"Well, I'm pretty good at putting my job at risk all by myself." I told him what happened today in Millie's office.

He raised his eyebrows and smirked. "Good. She needed to be put in her place."

"Yeah, but I've been the crazy one this whole time. She's been here with you, and I've been with—" I swallowed the hard knot growing inside my throat. "I've been with a ghost."

He chuckled. "It's okay."

I stared at him, wide-eyed. "How can you be okay with this? Look at you?"

He looked at himself for a few seconds. "I've had days to come to terms with everything. That's why it took me a while to even come around, and when I saw you at the gym, I was scared you'd find out everything and leave me."

"I'd never leave, especially when you need me."

He reached for my hand. And now I was holding his real hand *and* his ghost hand. The situation made

172

me want to laugh and cry at the same time. "After the accident, something inside told me you are the only one who can help me."

"What about Joe and Jasmine. Why didn't they call me?"

He shrugged. "Honestly, they haven't come to see me very often. I think they don't have any hope I'll recover. But somehow, I know everything's going to be okay."

My mind drifted back to Millie. What if she knew he was aware? Would she trust me so we could work together? It was worth a chance if she had any pull in the matter. Her dad was in high places. And I did have connections with Mary at the hospital. Maybe she could help me figure out a way to save him.

I squeezed both his hands. "I don't know where to start, but I'm the right girl for the job. I won't give up until I find a way."

Monday morning started like a twinge in my gums that developed into a toothache by lunch. It was all I could do to keep up with all of Millie's requests. She wanted me by her side constantly and wanted to be within arm's length of me at all times.

"Order this. Make sure he doesn't make me overpay. Call this person. I need this done now." All these demands were made with verbal exclamation points. Millie was just as concerned about the color of her napkins as she was about the waiters serving in the banquet area.

And all this had nothing to do with helping Cam.

Even though I'd been glued to the chair in Millie's office, I hadn't found the right words to say to her. It was as if the conversation last Friday hadn't happened, and everything was running as normal. Well Millie-normal.

I had spent all weekend brainstorming with Cam and never leaving his side, but it didn't matter. All I could do was sit there and talk or listen. Spending time together took on a whole new meaning for us, and I didn't want to waste a single minute.

Jasmine finally called me back on Sunday. She was in tears as she apologized. "If I would have known you didn't know, I would have called you back in a heartbeat. But I thought you did know, and Joe and I have been in denial that everything has happened the way it has."

"Well, you're going to love this," I said, with less enthusiasm. "Millie has been planning their wedding. She thinks that, after the thirty days, they're going to get married."

"What?" Jasmine screeched into the phone.

"Yep. It's supposed to happen the first week in December."

"But that's when they were originally supposed to get married. Has she been thinking they've been together this whole time? Because I can assure you, he broke up with her way before he met you."

I nodded. "I believe you. But she is sick in the head, I am sure of it. She has this delusion that when he wakes up from his coma, he'll forget they even broke things off."

Jasmine clucked her tongue. "Well, Joe and I won't let him do this to himself. If—*when* he wakes up, we'll be sure to clue him in."

I sighed and held the phone tighter against my ear. "So you think he'll wake up?"

Her voice broke as she fumbled with her words. "Yes, I do. I'm not giving up on him, and neither should you, Rory."

Her phone call had lifted me, giving me the strength I needed to be brave at a time of uncertainty. I always kept it together in front of Cam, wanting to be strong, but I lost it every night as I left him behind.

After work on Monday, I went straight to the hospital. Ghost-Cam was standing by the window when I came in. He turned, a worried expression on his face.

"Hey, what's going on?" I said, coming up to him. I reached out to hug him but my hands went right through him.

His frown deepened. "It's starting. I'm starting to lose my ghost form."

I tried to show a brave face instead of freaking out like my body wanted to do. "I'm sure it's nothing. Let's go to talk to Mary and see if we can't do something to slow things down and give you more time."

He nodded and followed me to the door.

But at the door, he groaned. I spun around to see him holding his hands against an invisible barrier. He mimed the space around the door. "I can't—I'm stuck."

"You mean, you can't leave the room?"

He nodded and backed up to the wall. He tried pushing through it, but it was as solid as it was for me.

Panic grew in his eyes. I went to him and held

both of his hands. "It's okay. I'll figure it out. Let me find Mary, and I'll be right back."

He shook his head. "Don't leave me."

I nodded. "Okay. I'll call her. I'll stay with you." I gave Mary a call on my cell, and she came right over. I sat on the bed next to the real Cam so it wouldn't seem so strange for her.

Mary came in the room, looking around suspiciously. "Is he here?"

I nodded and pointed to the window he'd been facing for the last few minutes. "He's lost his ability to move between walls. He's stuck in here."

Mary kept her eyes on the window but came closer. She checked something on one of his machines and made a clucking noise with her tongue.

"What?" I asked. "What does that mean?"

"His vitals," she said, pointing to his screen. "They're not as good as yesterday. Since he's been here, he's been pretty stable. Then on Friday, when you were here, they dropped a little." She found his chart and skimmed through it. Meanwhile, my mind whirled at all of the horrible possibilities. Did this mean he was dying?

Had showing up to see Cam in real life actually made things worse?

"Yeah, this is the first real decline he's had," she said, tapping on his chart.

Cam spun around, his face more solemn than I had ever seen. "Ask her if she can stop it from happening."

I nodded. "He wants to know if we can extend his care beyond his time limit."

She shook her head slowly. "He knows this. When

his time is up, legally, we can't make any exceptions."

Cam nodded and faced the window again. My heart thumped painfully in my chest.

"Thanks, Mary."

She nodded and headed to the door. Then she turned toward the window. "I'm really sorry, Cam. I hope our girl can find you a way out."

Cam remained quiet after Mary left. I didn't know what to say. What were you supposed to say to someone who knew death was waiting on their doorstep and they couldn't do anything about it?

"Do you want me to go?" I said after a minute.

I couldn't see his face, but I saw him nod. His voice sounded downtrodden and beaten. "Maybe that's for the best."

My heart fell in my chest. I wanted to lose it right then and there, but I forced myself to be strong. I cleared my throat. "I'll be back tomorrow. I'm not giving up on you. On us."

He continued to stare out the window, but said, "Thank you. I knew you wouldn't."

The next day after lunch, Millie found me huddled in my tiny office with a bottle of headache medicine.

"I'm leaving," she said, "but make sure everything we talked about is taken care of. Also, check out the email I sent about tomorrow's responsibilities. By the end of this week, I want this wedding all planned, just in case he... snaps out of things."

"You can't let them kill him." The words were out before I could stop them. I shrank in my desk chair,

177

waiting for her to yell.

She opened her mouth, then slammed it shut. For once she was speechless. I took the opportunity to spill the truth, or as much of it as I felt I could.

"I know about Cam now. I have a close friend at the hospital who told me about his accident, and I see him often."

Her eyebrows came together in a tight line. "You've been seeing him?"

She didn't need to know more about my past relationship with Cam than was strictly necessary. "Just in the hospital."

Millie stepped forward. "It's you, isn't it?" She narrowed her eyes and seemed to see me for the first time.

An uncomfortable shiver crawled down my back as she scrutinized me with her eyes. "What are you—"

She held her pointer finger at me. "No, don't do that. Don't sit there and pretend like there is nothing between you two. I can see it now. The other day, you knew about the fake wedding."

"So you admit it?" I said, challenging her.

"Oh, shove a cork in it." She tapped the side of her face. "Oh, how could I have missed this? You met him during Joe's accident, and I should've known then that you'd fall for him. Before his accident, he said he had moved on, met someone else."

"I didn't know that Cam—"

"His name is Phillip. And he's still mine. He may be in a coma right now, but when he wakes up, I'm convinced he'll forget all about you and about our little breakup. We've survived more than a little distraction." She glared at me one last time before turning her attention to her nails.

I glared right back. "You said it yourself. You're not together anymore."

She gritted her teeth, working her jaw a little. Her eyes flashed, making her mascara-heavy lashes look like the beginning of a cave or the doors to hell. "We will be together, don't you worry about that. And don't think that just because you have this little connection with him that you can bail on me now. Oh no, I will ruin you if you so much as sabotage or hinder this wedding from happening. Do you understand?"

I swallowed down the lump growing in my throat. "Perfectly."

She straightened up and plastered on a smile. "Well, since you know him so well, you'll get the measurements just right. He can't be uncomfortable on his big day."

I frowned. "Sure, I can run down to the hospital to make sure they're just right, but if he doesn't make it, it will be all for nothing."

Millie slammed her purse down on my desk, vibrating it with an awful thump. "Uh, no. You absolutely won't go see Phillip at the hospital. Those days are over."

My chest rose and fell as I tried to think of any shred of evidence that could prove we were together and they weren't, and that would persuade her not to bar me from seeing him. My shoulders fell, bringing a smile to her face. "You can't stop me from seeing him," I said, trying not to make it sound as weak as I felt.

Millie glared at me with her clumpy eyelashes. "Watch me."

I tried another angle. "Well, how else do you expect me to get the perfect measurements? I need to actually measure him."

Millie shook her head and looked back at her papers. "You're creative. Think of something else. If I see you at the hospital with him, I'll fire you."

I bristled and found my courage again. "Cam is not property. He's not something to be owned. Cam broke up with you weeks before his accident, and you're about as engaged as I am."

She huffed. "That you know of. Did he ever talk about me? Tell you we were engaged? That we own property together?"

I shifted to my other foot. "Yes, he did. The night of our first date."

"Oh, how cute," she said, smirking. "How about a second date? How did that go?"

I glanced around the room, hoping he'd appear in my tiny office and feed me the right things to say. Every other visit we had afterward had been when he was in the coma, and I couldn't really prove anything.

"It doesn't matter. Our relationship is none of your business."

"Exactly my point. My relationship with *my* fiancé is none of your business. You will do your job, or you can pack up your stuff tonight." She picked up her purse from her desk and with a resolute voice, said, "You'll have to get his measurements without seeing him. Get used to it. If he does wake up, I'll make sure he never sees you again."

I gulped. Cam's pleading thoughts came to my mind. I was the only one who could save him. "What if he doesn't wake up?"

She continued to pick at her cuticles, like she was trying to pick out whatever was wedged in them. "Well, then I guess I will feel satisfied I was the last person he loved."

My heart fell. She was right again. Cam and I had known each other for such a short time. "So, you're not going to do anything?"

She sighed in exasperation. "There's nothing I can do. It's not like he's appearing to you and me, telling us to fight for him."

I clamped my mouth shut. There was no way I was sharing the intimate details of my relationship with Cam. Especially not to her.

"Exactly. Now, get your head out of the clouds and focus on your job." She turned and left.

I ground my teeth together as I watched her disappear down the hall. I held a finger to my temple and tried to slow my thumping heart. Whenever I thought of losing Cam, never seeing his handsome face again, my chest physically hurt.

If she wasn't going to fight for him, I would. We had twelve days left, and I would find a way to save him. I had to.

Chapter 21

That night, I brought my laptop to the hospital with me. I waited until after eight o'clock, when Mary texted me that Millie went home and then snuck into his room. I shut the shades on his window just in case any passersby saw me talking to the invisible ghost version of Cam.

"Are you actually tiptoeing?"

I spun around at the sound of Cam's voice. He was standing by the window that faced the mountain, a serene look on his face. "Mary said she hasn't stopped by, but I just wanted to make sure—"

"She didn't come visit today." He frowned, and my breath caught for a second. Did he miss her? "You must've told her."

I stared into his blue eyes, hoping he didn't hate me for telling her so soon. "I did. I was hoping she might have some pull in stopping things from happening, but . . ." I trailed off, not wanting to repeat what she'd said. He seemed down enough without needing to hear more of her crazy delusions.

"Worth a shot. It was nice to have a break from her." The smile returned, and he motioned for me to sit on the bed.

"You don't want me to sit by you? I mean, I guess this *is* you," I said motioning to his comatose self.

He shrugged. "When I hold your hand, I can feel you, but when you hold my real hand, I feel warmth."

I nodded and sat next to him on the bed, balancing the laptop on my legs. Reaching for his hand, I watched his face for a reaction, but there was no change. Cam's ghost sat across from me on the bed and for a second, I wasn't sure where to rest my attention. I finally decided on my laptop. It was a safe medium.

"I brought my computer, hoping I could find some resources on how to help wake a comatose patient, or to reunite a spirit with its body. It may sound hokey, but so is talking to a ghost." After turning on my computer and linking to the hospital's guest internet connection, I finally dared a glance at him.

Ghost-Cam was studying me, a small grin on his face.

"What?" I asked. There was nothing more unsettling than a man smiling at you for no reason.

His grin grew a little. "Nothing. I'm just so happy you're here. That you're on my team."

I sighed. "Are you scared?"

He shrugged. "A little, but I can't do any more than I'm doing right now. Plus, if I do wake up, I'll have to marry Millie." My eyes snapped up to his, and he laughed. "Joking. I'm only joking. Lighten up. Somehow with you here, I know everything will be alright."

His reassurances did nothing for the mounting anxiety growing inside me. I'd rather see him marry Millie than die in a coma any day. But if I could do something about it, I would. I opened a search engine and typed in a key phrase: How to wake a man from a coma.

My eyes scrolled down the page, then jerked to a stop. "Have you had a PET scan? It measures how much sugar has eaten your brain cells, and it can indicate if you are in a total coma or a vegetative coma."

Cam crossed his hands behind his head and leaned back against the bed's headboard. "I am sure I have. If I was a vegetable, they would have cut me off sooner."

I clicked back to the main search and chose another article. After skimming the article, I said, "Having people talk to you and touch you is good. I can call your family, if you want."

"No," he said, deadpanning. "My parents were the only close family I had. I may have a few aunts and uncles somewhere but I'm not close enough to them for it to make a difference."

"What about Joe and Jasmine?"

He laughed. "Jasmine came last week and shooed Millie away for the night. She talked to me for forever about work and Joe. She says she's been avoiding calling you. So I guess I'm apologizing for her. She and Joe are really struggling."

"Maybe I'll call her instead. How about someone

at the hospital? Were you close to anyone?"

Cam sighed and reached across the bed for my free hand. His hands were noticeably colder. "This is one reason I waited so long to tell you. If you would've known this whole time, we'd have spent our time worrying and not flirting." He waggled his eyebrows, making me laugh. "See, that's what I really need."

I squeezed both of his hands and then released the one belonging to the ghost version. "Okay, I get it. You're right. It's probably good you didn't tell me sooner." I clicked back to the main search page for a last look, then smiled when I accidentally clicked on the images portion of the search engine. I hovered over the first image and then blushed when I realized what it was.

"What?" he said, coming to stand behind me. His cool hands held my shoulders lightly as he peeked at the screen. He laughed, pulling me closer to his chest. "Well, it did wake up Sleeping Beauty."

I closed my eyes, relishing his touch. "It's silly, I know. But I'd try if you wanted me to." I laid the laptop on the bed and turned to face him. His face was so close I could've done it then and there.

He lifted my chin with one hand and caressed my cheek with the other. "When we kiss for the first time, I want it to be real. I want to be present."

I frowned and crossed my arms. "But what if that never happens?"

He pouted his lips. "Why are you so doom and gloom today? Didn't you hear me? Somehow I know everything will be fine." He dropped his hands and pulled me back against his chest.

I breathed in his smell, but I didn't catch a whiff of

almond or cologne like I once had. Maybe my mind refused to acknowledge he was real. That's because he wasn't really there. I pushed back, retrieving my laptop from the bed. He already said I worried too much. Tears would be a buzzkill, so I needed to get out of there before my face started to leak my worries. "I need to go."

He nodded. "I tried to visit you at work today, but it seems like the closer we get to the wire, the more constrained I am here."

I sniffed. "It's okay. I have enough to worry about there."

He covered my hands with his cold fingers. "It'll be alright."

Man, I'd done it again. I was supposed to be helping here, not making things worse. "Sure. I'll see you tomorrow."

I reached back and squeezed his real hand, then headed for the door to make a quick exit. Before I could leave, he said, "Check on Swordy for me, will you? Stay there if you want."

I nodded, then turned back to the door as my eyes filled with tears.

"Oh, and Rory," I stood still, but stayed facing the door, "I hid my journal in the closet. There's something in there you need to read. Maybe it will help."

I squeezed his hand one last time before leaving. "I'll be back soon."

And then I left him, sitting on the side of the bed, staring at himself.

Chapter 22

On my way over to Cam's house, I called Jasmine. Her phone was turned off, so I left her a detailed message.

"I know about Cam. I know you two are hurting. Call me, girl, and let's eat a pint of ice cream together."

I hung up right as I turned down Cam's street. I felt empty inside, going without him. When I got to Cam's house, a lady with ink-black, braided hair was leaving. It was his housekeeper. I ducked around the corner of the house.

"Rory, is that you?"

I took a deep breath. She knew my name? I peeked around the side of the house to see her with her hands on her hips. She didn't look like a typical maid. She had long, dark, curly hair and wore gold rings and earrings and reminded me of a wealthy gypsy. Cam must have paid her extremely well.

"I knew it must've been you when I didn't see Millie's car," she said.

I looked back to the driveway where I'd parked. Why did I think I could hide? "Uh, yeah. You must be Maria. Cam told me about you . . . you know, before his accident," I added.

She crossed herself. "Poor man. Yes he told me about you too. I figured the note about Swordy must be from you or Jasmine. I don't know why he dated that witch for so long."

Another confirmation that they weren't together and it wasn't just Ghost-Cam telling me so. "Wait, he talked about me?"

She nodded and led me inside. "Not much, but enough that I knew something had changed about him." She paused and looked at her watch. "I was just on my way out. Do you need anything?"

"I came to feed Swordy."

She nodded, but kept a sharp eye on me. "Well, if Cam trusts you, so do I."

I breathed a sigh of relief and, after a quick goodbye, fled to Cam's room. Swordy was happy to see me, bumping his nose against the glass as I fed him.

Just then, the front door slammed shut. "Maria, are you here?"

I crossed the room and opened the door right as Millie's voice echoed around me. Panic struck me like a knife in my nerves. I stood there, completely paralyzed.

"Maria, are you here?" She waited a few seconds and then said, "Good. I hate it when you're here anyway. Whose car *is* here, though?"

I forced myself to move and peeked out the door to see Millie coming toward me up the stairs. She walked fast and there was no time to hide. How could I explain being here? I ran for his closet and hid among his shirts.

The whole closet smelled like him, sending a wave of desire over me. Oh, I missed him so much. I reached up for one of his shirts and breathed in. Then I had an idea and walked out of the closet, right into the pathway of Millie.

Millie was just about to open the closet door when I waltzed out and had to do a double take. "What are you doing here?" she said forcibly. "I told you—"

"You told me not to see him. I'm not technically seeing him by going to his house." I held up the shirt. "You said you wanted me to be creative, right? Well, here is his shirt with the right measurements. All I have to do is bring this to the tuxedo shop to find the right match."

Millie brushed past me, positioning herself before all of his clothes.

The floor underneath Millie's foot creaked as she tapped her toe. "Hmm, how resourceful. Well before you go all Nancy Drew, I need to gather some of his clothes for work and switch out some old ones. He looks so much better in regular clothes than he does in that hideous hospital gown."

And he did. Seeing him in a hospital gown would have made things harder.

She sighed and brought the handful of clothes to her nose. She breathed into them, her eyes softer than they'd ever been. "I really miss him."

I swallowed down the lump in my throat. My body turned cold and numb as embarrassment flooded my veins. What was I doing? Dating an almost-married, comatose man? I felt like a homewrecker. And instead of Millie being the evil one, I was the one in the wrong.

"I'll make sure we get his measurements just right."

Millie turned to me, her eyes hardening a little. "Yes, see that they are perfect." She spun around and exited his room, leaving me feeling hopeless.

I waited until I heard the front door close before I breathed a sigh of relief. Then, remembering why I was here, I got on my knees and checked the floor, in the exact spot Millie had stood. Nowhere in Cam's house did the floors creak. Except here. Was it a faulty floor? The carpet shifted, a little smaller than the floor, and I reached down and pulled up the patch of carpet he had used to cover a hole, revealing a hidden latch-door in the wooden floor. My heart thumped. Even in ghost form, he had been telling the truth.

The door lifted easily, revealing a space the size of a shoebox. Inside was a burgundy, leather-bound book. I opened it up to see a mostly blank journal. He had only written a few entries. Even though his handwriting was tempting, these entries would have to wait for later. I wanted the privacy of my own house, just in case Millie decided to come back.

I gave Swordy one last tap on the glass, held the journal tightly to my chest, and then hurried outside. The sun had been out before but now was replaced by a half moon. The stars shone all around me, and if I hadn't been in such a hurry to get out of there, I would have stayed to appreciate it.

My hands shook as I headed back home. Right then, I felt like giving up. I had no business getting into his and Millie's relationship. And if Cam woke up and had no knowledge of us, I didn't know what I'd do. So many hard questions I had no answers to.

I forced myself to get ready for bed once I got home. It was torture going through the motions of brushing my teeth and changing knowing that journal was waiting, but finally I was in bed and ready to read. Then, and only then, did I allow myself to open his journal. My hands shook as I turned the first page and read.

Feb. 3

> *Something doesn't feel right. I don't know how long I've felt this way, probably since I moved to Mount Shasta. I love my job, I love being by the mountains again and spending time with Joe. I think I still love Millie, but it's getting harder to tell. I just don't know if I made the right decision by investing in the resort.*

So this had been a long time in coming. I flipped a page and read the next few entries without stopping.

Feb. 16th

> *Valentine's Day was kind of a blow this year. To put a spark back into our relationship, I planned a romantic dinner, doing all the things Millie loves. An Italian restaurant a few hours away, a private ride in a 5-seater plane, and a relaxing massage waiting for her back at the*

house. I even told Millie to plan ahead and take the whole day off, that I'd be spoiling her. She was thrilled at first, and I thought this would smooth over the last few weeks.

Two hours before we were supposed to leave, Millie claimed a disaster happened at the resort and she couldn't come but to go ahead without me. I called the resort a few hours later to check on her and see if I couldn't bring her lunch, but the resort claimed there had been no disaster and Millie hadn't come in to work. Just to make sure, I drove over there myself and checked her office. Empty and dark.

At first, I thought maybe she had been planning something on the side and hadn't let me know, but when I returned home alone, all was quiet. She didn't answer any of my calls and her car was missing from her apartment. I confronted her about it today and she claimed she went home with a headache, but I know she was lying. I don't know what to believe, but I know I don't feel the same way about her. I'm just not sure how we can get around this.

Mar. 27th

It's been a long month, full of busy days at the hospital. They've kept me busy, so happy to have a doctor that plans on sticking around. With ski season ending soon, things should slow down, but I kind of like the long hours. It keeps my mind off of what's really happening between

Millie and me. Which is nothing.

May 15th

> *I'm growing restless with the situation at the resort. Millie has started to change the time and dates of the board meetings, so I have no idea how the resort is doing. She has closed me out of all the financial situations, and right now, I think it's best I keep my distance. We meet each other for dinner occasionally throughout the week, and sometimes catch a movie if things are going well, but things are becoming very platonic between us. I am not sure I care.*

I kept reading, each entry describing his restlessness with Millie and the situation at the resort, and, by the end, I was convinced that his relationship with Millie had deteriorated long before we even met. The journal was not even half full. Despite his medical-scrawl handwriting, I read through each entry, laughing at some of the adventures he had at work, like the time he had slipped on a bed pan and the charge nurse had seemed out to get him ever since, and weeping with him as he expressed a desire to not be alone in a relationship where the other person viewed him as a pawn in a game.

He occasionally had adventures with Joe and Jasmine, but the further into the journal I read, the less I saw about them. He mentioned his break up with Millie on October 13th, and then the journal ended. I felt disappointed, despite learning that his relationship had ended. If nothing else, reading his journal had confirmed that. But we hadn't met until the end of October. So much could have happened in between that time.

I flipped through the remaining pages and gasped when I saw the beginning of an entry, hidden later in the journal. My heart raced as I read the date.

Oct. 23rd

The date we met. My eyes flew across the page hungrily.

> *I met the most beautiful woman today. Her name is Rory and unfortunately, she works at the resort Millie and I own. Joe got in a ski accident, and, instead of taking care of it herself, Millie sent Rory to do her dirty work. I feel bad yelling at her for neglecting Joe. She stood up to me though, and once I realized it was at Millie's resort where he'd had the accident, I felt like a bonehead. I had attacked her for no good reason.*

> *Turned out, Jasmine knew Rory from high school and arranged for all four of us to meet for dinner, which was perfect, because I didn't know how or if I could ask her out after the way I treated her. She wasn't a patient, but I did meet her at the hospital. After Rory frankly forgave me and spent the night making me laugh, I knew she was different. I've been so absorbed with Millie for so long, I didn't know I could be happy again.*

But I got scared toward the end of the night and told her I wasn't ready for anything. She probably didn't see me as anything other than another guy, but I can't stop thinking about her. I have to see her again.

The entry ended suddenly, and I flipped the page to see if another one followed, but this was it. There were no more entries. This was the only hint I had that he felt something more for me. I closed my eyes and took a breath.

Here was the proof I needed to show me this wasn't all in my head. He felt for me the way I felt for him. Maybe not love, but he had been interested. There was still a good chance that even if he did wake up, he wouldn't remember me. Plenty of people lost memories when they had brain injuries, and we had so few to rely on. Two dates was hardly a foundation for a relationship.

I collapsed against my bed, weary with my thoughts. What was I going to do when his time was up?

Chapter 23

The final days before Millie's possible wedding and Cam's deadline were some of the worst since the week of my parent's funeral. One thought hammered in my head: if he did make it, how would he feel about waking up to a prepared wedding?

I had visited Cam every night until last night. Last night, he disappeared altogether and I was only left with his comatose form. But today was the day. Today, they would be releasing Cam of all care at 4:00 PM if there was no change in his health status.

Brittney tried to cheer me up at work, helping out with anything she could while juggling all of her new responsibilities, but it did nothing for my mood. I was in a funk. Planning Millie's wedding had become a chore, and, halfway through the day, I couldn't pretend anymore. Today, I needed to be with Cam.

Before I left, I found Millie in the banquet area, inspecting the decorations I had spent all day putting up.

"I need to talk to you," I said, inwardly cursing how weak my voice sounded.

She crossed her arms, but kept her eyes on the garland wrapped around each column. "What is it now?"

I clasped my hands tightly in front of me. "I need to resign from my responsibilities. Brittney would be a better match for pulling off this wedding. Everything is already planned, I just can't . . . I'm happy to take my old responsibilities back, but I can't help you with this event anymore."

Millie looked back at Brittney, who stood at the door, waiting in case she was needed, then moved her glare to me. "No, you're going to do this. I want you to be there when he says 'I do'. To *me*."

I swallowed hard. "There will be no wedding if a miracle doesn't happen tonight."

Millie laughed. "If he doesn't wake up, then I guess he'll die engaged to me. Just the way it should be. And the shares he had—" she gritted her teeth and went through great efforts to maintain her smile— "has... were never turned over to anyone. They're still in his name. After he resigned at the board meeting, I ripped them up, knowing he would change his mind later and regret it. And when he dies, those shares become mine."

I inhaled sharply, making her evil grin grow wider. "How could you do that to him? He loved you. He cared about you."

She sniffed, and her confidence wavered for a few

seconds. But just as quickly, her face returned to its stoic position. "Daddy thought I could do better, and I think I agree. Though Phillip will have to do for as long as I need him. It's laughable that you thought he would be interested in you."

"You're heartless," I snapped, unable to bear the charade any longer. My legs felt weak, and tears were fast gathering in my eyes. I needed to get out of there fast, before I made the situation worse.

"Oh, quit your crying. Chances are Phillip won't make it anyway. But, no. You're not done with this job until I say you are. If you leave, I will destroy this place."

My breath faltered. "Seriously?"

"Oh, yes. I just was looking at the ownership papers the other day. It seems that your dead parents used to own this place when it was more of a shack. If you go anywhere, I will ruin you and this place that you love. I'll be sure to sell this perfect space of land to developers that have been biting at my heels for months."

I balled my fists together, pinching the skin on my palms so tightly I felt blood. I reared my hand back and struck, popping her right in the eye. She fell with a grunt, holding her face with her hands and moaning in pain.

"You hit me!" she screeched, her voice stunned. "You . . . you . . . just wait until Phillip finds out!" Her voice trembled as she shook her fist at me.

Gathering all the courage I had left in me, I gave her what I hoped was a withering glare. "His friends call him Cam."

I spun on my heel as she cursed at my back. I fled

to my office to grab my things and headed for my car. If I didn't have a job on Monday morning, I'd be okay with that.

Now for the harder part of my day.

All the way to the hospital, I thought of what I'd say to Millie if she came to Cam's room. I wasn't going to leave no matter what happened. If he only had a few hours to live, I was going to stay with him until the end.

Luckily, all my rehearsing had been in vain. Only one nurse was in Cam's room. She was petite and stood on her tiptoes to check his IV.

"Hi, come on in," she said. "Glad someone is here to see this man off."

I cringed. How crass could she be?

She must've taken my silence as agreement because she kept right on talking. "It's too bad too, because his color has returned a little."

"Really?" I said. I came over to his bedside, pulling a chair behind me. Even though there was a little more color in his cheeks, his oxygen mask still pumped air for him.

The nurse left the room after a minute, and I whispered to him. "Cam, are you here?" When Ghost-Cam did not appear and only his limp, real form remained, I reached for his hand and squeezed, bringing it to my lips. "I'd do anything to hear your voice, just one last time." I whispered my plea so softly that I could barely hear the words myself.

I would bargain anything to keep him alive.

When nothing happened after a few minutes, I squeezed his hand. It was now or never. Soon, Millie would be arriving, and I would lose this opportunity to tell him how I felt. I cleared my throat and prayed for a few minutes of uninterrupted silence.

"Cam, this has been the worst week of my life. I've missed you every day and every moment. Planning your wedding with Millie has been a nightmare. But if you live, if you wake up, I'll attend your wedding with a smile on my face."

My throat tightened as I thought of how I could say the next part. "I don't know if the moments I had with you were real, or how you really feel, but after getting to know you and care about you, I can honestly tell you how I feel."

I told him of some of the happy times we spent together, remembering the confusing moments, the moments of shock when I found out the truth. It had been a whirlwind of a relationship, but I wouldn't have had it any other way. I talked to him for over an hour before a medical team started gathering outside. Before they came in, I shared my last few thoughts with him.

"I have never loved someone like I have loved you. You have filled this aching gap in my life I didn't know how to fill. You probably saved my life that one day outside the hospital, and that is the type of man I want to spend forever with. I'm here for you."

The door swung open, and I sat back in my seat. A group of doctors came in, followed by Joe, Jasmine, and Millie. Joe and Jasmine smiled at me while Millie's face remained stoic, though her eye was purpling up nicely.

As the doctors moved around us to do one more examination, we watched quietly. My throat constricted so much that, if I had tried to speak, my words would have come out in strained screeches.

Jasmine and Joe kept giving Millie hateful glances, but she kept her eyes averted from anyone but Cam. Finally, the main doctor started talking, and everything else was forgotten.

Things went fast after that. The doctors began speaking, walking us through the steps of his final release. One doctor started removing equipment around his mouth. Every sound tore at my ears, and I pinched my eyes closed so I didn't have to see it happening.

Jasmine reached over and took my hand. "Honey, we're here. We'll help you through."

Millie snapped her head up, her purple eye glinting maliciously. "I can't believe you're even in here."

Joe moved to my side. "Rory deserves to be here more than you. He loved her."

I raised my head, staring into Joe's eyes. How did he know? We'd only known each other a few days.

"He loved you, Rory," he said again. "He called me after he left your house that night. I was on the phone when—" His voice broke, and he put his face in his hands.

Jasmine tucked an arm around him and hugged him tightly. "It'll be okay."

Tears streamed down my face, and my voice faltered. "Why? Why is this happening?"

A doctor came forward. "We're sorry, but it's time. If Cam's organs are to be donated, we have to move quickly. We will release him of his oxygen aid, and if he does not recover within a few minutes, our directive is not to resuscitate him, but to donate all vital organs. Please step back while we finish this procedure."

"Wait, just one more second," I called out. I ran to Cam's side. Everyone was looking at me, but I didn't care. I stepped as close to him as I could and leaned in so we could have a more private moment.

Trying not to mess anything up, I lifted his oxygen mask and kissed him, right on the mouth. It was our first and last kiss. It was quick and simple, but it was all I could give him. A tear fell on his cheek, and I wiped it away tenderly.

"I love you."

I backed away and watched in horror as the doctor removed the tape holding the tube running through his nose and took the oxygen away from his mouth. Immediately, my eyes focused on the monitor screen, praying for a miracle.

Please wake up, Cam. Please.

The heart monitor beeped faster, showing a decreasing heart rate. A minute passed and still his heart rate continued to slow. The beeping became erratic, and the alarm on the machine sounded. A nurse turned it off, and we continued to watch the red flickers barely present on the monitor.

I squeezed Jasmine's hand and looked to the ceiling. A spark of an idea came to me, and I hated myself for even thinking it. But if it worked, I wouldn't care. It would be worth it.

Please. I'll do anything. I'll let Millie have him. I will leave Cam alone if he'll just wake up.

Suddenly, the heart monitor started to beep again. The doctors around us inhaled a breath as Cam coughed and sputtered his first word. "Water."

I sobbed into my hands at the sound of his voice, and the rest of the room seemed to sigh together.

A doctor held up a hand to silence us, but after a few seconds of checking Cam's heart and his alert response, he spoke. "Hi, my name is Doctor Ramsey."

"I know you are," Cam said hoarsely. "I know who you are. I know where I am, though I'm not sure how I got here. I'll tell you more once you give me water."

Dr. Ramsey chuckled and turned to the nurse.

She gave him a few sips of water before he sighed.

"Ok, now continue with the drill," Cam said.

Doctor Ramsey smiled patiently. "Cam, you were in a car accident. You fell into the canyon, and you've been in a coma for thirty days."

"Thirty days!" Cam said. "Were you about to cut me off?"

Dr. Ramsey nodded. "You are very lucky, and you're showing excellent response so far. We still have to do some neuro tests, but the prognosis is hopeful so far."

Joe, Jasmine, and I turned to each other, crying tears of happiness.

"Do you remember anything about the accident?"

Cam shook his head.

Dr. Ramsey nodded. "Tell me the last thing you do remember?"

"I-I remember proposing to Millie. And the resort. And work."

Millie turned to me and sneered. "See?" she whispered so only the three of us could hear.

We waited patiently as the doctors continued their examinations, listening to bits and pieces of what he could remember.

Another one of the doctors, Dr. Hill, turned to us, a grim look on her face. "Coma patients are very sensitive when they can't remember things. Take care not to overwhelm him if his memory is not quite all there. Sometimes it takes weeks, months, even years for a full recovery. Sometimes, the memories never return."

"And what if he does remember something perfectly, like our wedding? It's scheduled for next week, and I was hoping we could continue with it."

Dr. Hill shrugged. "If he is agreeable and is fit to come, I see no problem with this."

Joe shook his head. "You are disgusting, Millie. You know just as well as we do that he broke up with you weeks before the accident."

She shook her head. "No, I don't remember that at all." Her voice darkened as she lowered her voice so we could only hear. "And bringing it up to him could seriously hurt him, so maybe it's best you leave."

"You have some visitors," Dr. Ramsey said, stepping back. Millie brushed past the three of us to kneel next to his bed.

My heart dropped to my feet. I couldn't fight for Cam even if I wanted to. Calling it a coincidence would have been too easy, but it wasn't. It was a miracle, and now, my part was done.

I leaned over to whisper to Joe and Jasmine. "Please don't mention anything to Cam about me. I think it's best if I go."

Joe's eyebrows knit together. "Wait, what? Don't go. Cam wants to see you."

Jasmine shook her head. "Why, girl? Don't let Millie scare you away. He'll remember you."

"It's not about that. I made a promise, and I've got to keep my distance."

"Just wait a few seconds," Jasmine said, pleading with her eyes. I nodded, but took a few steps back.

"Millie? Are we still . . . engaged. Are we getting married?"

She laughed and kissed his forehead. My heart felt like it could leap and decompose at the same time. "Yes, of course. An accident couldn't keep us apart," Millie said.

I winced. *She's got him under her spell once more.*

She smiled and leaned forward to kiss his lips.

"Who hit you in the eye?" he asked before she could make contact.

I avoided Millie's eyes, but I could feel her irritation. "No one gave me this," she said, grinding her teeth together.

Jasmine looked at me, and I gave her a little nod. She bumped my shoulder and gave me a thumbs-up.

Millie flinched as he reached out to touch her face. "It was an unfortunate accident at work, but I'll take care of it. My eye should be back to normal in a few days."

Cam turned his focus to the three of us. "Joe, Jasmine, you're here."

"Hey, buddy," Joe said. He and Jasmine joined Cam on the other side of the bed, facing Millie and I. I was alone, standing in perfect sight of him.

My heart thumped, overflowing with emotion. I loved this man.

"You gave us a big scare," Joe said.

Jasmine tapped his arm, much lighter than I'd seen her tap Joe. "Don't do that again. I already have one walking disaster. I don't need two."

Cam actually smiled. The two of them spoke with him for a moment, and then his eyes turned on me.

"Do you remember Rory?" Jasmine asked Cam.

Millie turned around. Her eyes flickered with hatred, but she didn't say anything.

I smiled, waiting with bated breath to see if he remembered anything. *Please remember something.*

Cam looked to Joe for help. "I'm sorry. I don't. Should I know her?"

Millie gave me a smug smile and stood so she could see both of us. "No, she's the help. In fact, you were just leaving, weren't you?" She lifted one eyebrow at me.

Joe looked to me with a pained expression, but I shook my head. "Millie's right. I was just concerned, and it looks like you are good now."

"Wait," Cam said, trying to sit up.

I stopped breathing so I could listen. *He remembered me?*

"You work at the resort, don't you? I think you work with my fiancée."

Millie laughed, her voice high and shrill. "She's the one that's planning our wedding."

My heart dropped like a rock in an empty well. *No, please. No!*

"How about a wedding here at the hospital next Tuesday? It was our original date, and I couldn't bear to call everyone back when—"

"When you dumped her," Joe said, his voice angrier and louder than I'd ever heard it. The nurse still in the room turned to us, her brows drawn in a worried frown.

206

Joe shook his head. "I'm sorry, but I am not going to sit here and watch you marry her. You dumped her weeks before your accident."

Cam scratched his head. "Wait, no. I'm with Millie. I'm marrying Millie."

His heart rate started to race, and the nurse came over, pushing Joe to the side. She checked his monitor and, a few seconds later, placed an oxygen mask on his face. "Whatever you're talking about, stop. It's putting stress on Dr. Camden, and we're not sure he hasn't had any permanent damage. His recovery could be set back if you agitate him. Maybe it's best if you all leave."

Millie nodded in agreement. "That will give you the weekend to recover, Sweetie. I can't wait another minute to be all yours."

Cam laid back against the pillow and held on to his mask, breathing deeply and looking confused. I looked at Jasmine, who was glaring at Millie.

"He shouldn't be making any decisions for his future right now," she snapped.

Joe nodded. "Cam, you don't need to decide anything now. Getting married is a big choice, and we want you to be sure you know who you're marrying."

Millie seemed to growl in response. "Phillip knows exactly who he's marrying. We've been engaged for a long time, and now it's time to make things official."

Cam nodded. "It's all right, Joe. I want to do this."

Joe shook his head, but didn't say anything else.

Millie leaned against Cam. "I'm sure you'll like what Rory's planned for us."

Cam met my eyes and smiled his swoon-worthy

smile. Even with an oxygen mask over his face, he was handsome. "I'm sure it's amazing."

I smiled, but inside, I deflated like a week-old balloon. "Well, I better be going. See you soon. I hope your recovery goes smoothly."

I left without saying goodbye and ran for the elevators as the room erupted into conversation behind me, Joe and Jasmine's voices the loudest of all.

The doctors must have kicked them out for being too loud because as I waited for the elevator, the three of them came out in the hallway and continued their argument. If nothing else, I hoped the two of them would convince Cam that Millie wasn't right for him.

For me it was over. It was finally over, and I could move on. Cam was alive, and that was enough for me.

Chapter 24

Mary, Rose, Dawn!" I cried, almost tripping over my own feet as I entered their house. The three of them ran to me, barely waiting until I'd closed the door behind me before they enveloped me in tight hugs.

"He didn't wake up?" Mary asked. Her face was etched with worry.

I nodded. "He did about an hour ago." I let the tears fall, finally allowing them to escape now that I was in the safety of the ninnies' arms.

Mary patted my shoulder. "That's great, honey. Why are you still so sad? Here, let's sit down, and you can tell us the whole story."

We moved our four-person hug to the couch and sat down, close and tight.

I sighed and started from the beginning, telling

them the new information I'd learned about Millie, then about how I'd punched Millie in the face and left work early.

Mary smiled at that part but didn't interrupt.

I sighed and wiped my face. "Well, I went in early to tell him how I felt before everyone else got there. I just wanted him to know that I felt the same way he did, well, before everything happened. I even took off his oxygen mask so I could kiss him goodbye, just in case he…" I stopped talking, not wanting to finish my sentence. I had come too close to losing him.

"You kissed him?" Dawn asked.

I nodded, blushing a little. "I was sure I'd mess everything up, but—"

"No," all three of them said at the same time.

"You kissed him awake," Mary said solemnly. "I've heard of it happening before, but not to someone in a coma."

"What a true miracle," Rose said. "You were meant to be together."

My chest tightened as I thought of the bargain I had made with a higher power. I started crying, and Rose gathered me closer in her arms. "He wasn't responding at first, and his breathing was slowly stopping, so I promised myself if he made it through all this, I would give him up. Millie could have him, and I would leave him alone."

"Oh no," Dawn said.

I nodded. "And then a few seconds later, he woke. It was a miracle. But then I knew I had to follow through with my promise. Who cares if we can't be together? I just want him to be alive."

Rose patted my hand. "So what happened then?

Did he remember you?"

"Well, I wasn't the only one who showed up to see his last moments. Millie, Joe, and Jasmine were there. He recognized Millie first, then Joe and Jasmine."

"But not you?"

I nodded. "He knew my name and that I worked with Millie. Oh," I said, remembering the worst part, "she has him convinced they are still engaged. His wedding will take place on Tuesday."

Mary's sympathetic smile slipped from her face. "But she can't do that. You have to talk to him. You must tell him the truth."

I shook my head. "I can't. Something worse could happen if I go back on my promise. And Joe, he tried to tell Cam he wasn't even dating her, and Cam lost it. He started breathing hard, and the nurse had to put an oxygen mask over his face."

Mary huffed and sat back against the couch. Her dark, quizzical brows twitched a few times on her forehead before she spoke. "I can't believe he believed her."

I shrugged. "Millie told him I was planning their wedding. So I can't back out now, can I?"

Rose cleared her throat. "Well, you could, honey. I know you've held onto your job for very sweet personal reasons, but your dad and mom would never be okay with someone treating you unkindly."

More tears slipped down my face. Why did they have to be gone? I wanted to hear their voices so badly.

"But," Rose continued, as if my stream of thoughts hadn't occurred, "if you walk away now, you'll never get closure to this situation. And though *you* made a

211

promise to stay away, there is no telling that *he* will. He fell for you once. He might again."

A spark of hope fluttered in my chest. Was he still the old Cam I fell in love with? There was no doubt in my mind how I felt, but that made this even worse. "But what if he does go through with it, and I have to watch him marry her?"

Mary grunted. "Builds character."

The four of us laughed, and it felt good to release the knot of tension that had been building inside.

Dawn folded her hands together in front of her. "It's okay, sisters. Everything will fall into place. Hold on to your hope."

I leaned against the couch and cried.

Rose stepped behind me on the couch, and pulled my hair back in a soothing gesture. "Come on ladies, let's fix some dinner. Rory, we'll give you a little time to yourself, but why don't you stay this weekend? We'd love to have you."

I nodded, not knowing if I even had strength to drive home.

Rose went into the kitchen to make her famous chicken noodle soup, while the other two sat in the kitchen, whispering to each other. I knew they were talking about me, but I didn't care. I had dug myself this giant hole, and now, I had to climb out. Even though the obvious answer was to pack up and quit, I wouldn't do it, if only for the fact that I wanted to see Cam one last time. Then I would leave my job and never look back. But for now, I would see this thing to the end, even if it broke my heart.

I spent the rest of the weekend at the ninnies' house. I didn't even go home to change. They cared for me as they would a sick child, and I let them.

I kept to myself, in the little spare bedroom I occasionally stayed in. I watched shows, I ate when food was brought, but mostly, I cried. I cried over a love I would never get to have again. At some point, I dragged myself out to the car to reread the journal entries. I'd put it there so I could have it close by whenever I needed it.

To release some of the anguish inside, I wrote my own entries, expressing since day one how I felt about Cam. It seemed right to write in the same book he'd written in. There, our feelings would always stay.

Right before bed on Sunday night, the ninnies invited me to leave my room and watch a show with them. It did nothing to distract me, but it was nice seeing different walls to stare at. My phone buzzed, and I scrambled to open it. I sighed as I looked at the sender's name.

The ninnies looked over in interest, and I read it through once and then summarized the message for their benefit.

"It's Millie. She wants to meet me at the hospital tomorrow to arrange the decorations. She warned me not to say anything about Cam or to even talk with him."

"Or what?" Mary demanded, crossing her arms.

"Or she'll fire me."

Mary guffawed. "Now wouldn't that just be the ticket? In my opinion, I'd say go for it. Who would ever

213

want to work with that witch anyway?"

I shrugged. Even though I didn't want to work with Millie anymore and had decided to turn in my advance notice, I still had two weeks of work left before I could leave.

Rose spoke up too. "Honey, I agree with Mary. You may have to keep your end of the bargain and leave Cam alone, but maybe helping him see that Millie is not right for him wouldn't cross any lines."

I glared at the text, trying to decide how to go about that. What if I told him and messed everything up? I sighed. Cam deserved better. I could leave him alone, but he had to at least know the truth, even if I couldn't tell it to him myself.

Chapter 25

Monday morning started with a bang. I came into the tiny hospital chapel right on time only for Millie to bite my head off about the room being too small.

I tried to start things off on the right foot. "Well, try to look on the bright side. We'll have less to decorate, less flowers to pay for, and a more intimate guest list. I gathered a lot of what we already put up, and there is a dining hall if you want us to set up your luncheon there."

Millie glared at me. "You think I want to eat in this disgusting place?"

I looked around to see who had overheard, but we were the only ones in the tiny chapel. "Well, then, I'll return what I can and cancel the food." As if she really cared what I did so long as I made it better for her. She was already on to criticizing the next thing.

"These pews are too small. How am I going to fit everyone from my guest list?" I turned around to estimate the amount of people we could fit . . . and froze.

It was Cam, and oh, he looked so good. Even in comfy clothes, he looked handsome. His color was back to normal, and everything looked the way it should, minus the IV still in his arm. A nurse had just pushed him up to the door in a wheelchair. His face brightened, though I wasn't sure if it was because of Millie or because of me. I pushed the fluttering feeling of hope way down to my feet where I mentally stomped it out of my body.

Millie faced me still, plopping down in one of the pews to sulk, not even noticing Cam behind her.

I quickly snapped my attention away from Cam. If she knew I held onto a spark of hope, this would all be over before I even had a chance.

I quickly scanned the pews and tried to give her an estimate of the number of people we could squeeze in. "I bet fifty could come. It's kind of a small venue, but we can make it work since you want it here."

"Fifty? I invited over five *hundred*. You think I wanted to have my wedding in this stupid hospital? I'm just doing it here so that Phillip is more comfortable. After tomorrow, he is mine. And you're going to sit there and watch it all happen."

I glanced up at Cam, who was watching me intently with a stern glare. A flush of heat ran to my face. What did he think of me? Was he irritated with me for making Millie upset?

He cleared his throat loudly.

Millie seemed to recognize Cam's voice and

216

immediately fixed her face and spun around. She walked over and sat in the pew next to his chair. "Oh, Phillip, you're here. Wait, didn't the nurse dress you? You can't get married in sweats tomorrow, silly." She tapped his nose.

He smiled a sneaky smile. "I know, I know. I'll make sure I'm ready."

If it wasn't Millie making him frown, it had definitely been me. I went to work, studying the room space I would have to work with. Much easier to decorate than a ballroom. But the smaller the amount of space, the more into detail Millie would be. I tried to block out their conversation, but the room echoed. It really was too small for private conversations.

"Are you going to stand up during the ceremony, or will I have to wheel you down the aisle?" Millie asked. She laughed, but by the look of Cam's face, I knew he was bothered.

"I'll sit for today," he said, a slight edge to his voice.

Millie planted her hands on her hips and puckered her lips in an unsatisfied way. "Well, okay. I guess I should be glad you're even here."

I glared at her, not caring if Cam saw or not. She noticed and decided to amend her statement. "I mean, I'm just glad to be marrying you tomorrow."

The rest of the day went like this. Awkward interactions between the two, and because I knew he had struggled with their relationship before I met him, I could now tell why. Millie was never happy. After an hour of sitting in the wheelchair while preparations went on around him, Cam bowed out with promises to return, and I busied myself with decorating the room the best I could. It was a tiny chapel with eight pews on either side. I had no idea how everyone would fit so I made sure to talk to someone who controlled the room's temperature.

The hospital was accommodating, but they were a care facility, not an events arena. When I tried to find someone to answer one of Millie's dozens of questions, they sent me to the third floor where the events manager's office was. It was empty. Completely empty, in fact. All that was left was an office desk with a chair. Not even a name tag.

I approached a lady with black, curly hair to her shoulders and motioned to the empty office. "Do you know where the event manager's office is? We are having a wedding tomorrow in the chapel, and I have a list of things to ask them."

She nodded toward the door I stood in front of. "You're looking at it." Withholding a sigh of frustration, I faced her again. She wore black slacks and a plain, green blouse that matched her eyes. She seemed older than me, but not by much. Her eyes sparkled, and she wore a coy smile.

"Sorry. That was rude," she said. "My name is Cassie. Regina was the manager, but she retired a month ago after being here for almost thirty years. I kind of took over her position until they find a new one, but I stink at it. We're trying really hard to fill it."

My eyebrows lifted. "What kind of events do you do?"

"Oh, all kinds. We use the chapel, of course you know, but only sparingly with patients. We have a few banquet areas that can be rented out."

"Really? Hospitals do that?" I asked.

"It's a little unusual, I know, but it brings in more money to the hospital and helps pay for the community gym that's downstairs. The big responsibility we have is arranging events for the staff. We would train this person in the type of events and meetings that the hospital staff regularly has. We cater most of the meetings, most of them with light snacks and drinks, but occasionally, the administration orders full dinners and we order from an outside caterer."

This might be the open door I was looking for after leaving Ski Ridge. "Are you looking to fill that position?" I asked her.

It was Cassie's turn to do some eyebrow lifting. "Would you be interested?"

I nodded, though inside my heart was breaking. "I might be."

She smiled. "Well I'd love to talk to you, maybe when you're not in the midst of one of your events, and for now, I'm happy to help you with whatever you need. I'll stick around and see how you work, and then maybe we can call this your tryout."

I deflated a bit. The thought of leaving the resort left me with an empty feeling. But, the ninnies were right. If I wasn't happy, would Mom and Dad really be happy for me? "Sounds great," I finally said. "My boss is a . . ."

"A piece of work?" she said, filling in the blank. "I know all about Millie. You don't have to explain a thing. I just feel bad that you've had to put up with her while she's been brainwashing Dr. Camden into marrying her again."

"So, you think so too?" I said, liking Cassie

already.

"Yes. We all love that guy. And man, is he hot! Geesh!"

I blushed and then realized I would give her the wrong idea. Even if Millie was a terrible boss, it wouldn't start a good precedent to be talking trash about her with my maybe-new boss. "I hope everything turns out okay for him. He's been through a lot."

Cassie nodded. "You know, right before his coma, the whole hospital saw a change in Cam. He was smiling, happy, and he told a couple of the patients he had met someone new."

I blushed again, and this time, Cassie noticed.

"It's not you, is it?"

I shrugged. "We went out a couple of times before his accident."

Cassie dragged me to a chair. "Oooh, spill fast! You have maybe five minutes until Millie comes looking for you. What happened?"

I sighed, but told her the digested version of the story as fast as I could in the few minutes I knew I had left. I left out a few details, like my ghostly visits with Cam, but gave her the big gist, up until the moment he woke up.

She paused, soaking in everything. Then she said, "So you're telling me that when Cam woke up, he didn't recognize you at all?"

I nodded. "Well, mostly. I left soon after he woke, but before I left, he remembered my name and that I worked with Millie."

Cassie sighed. "Well, that's a start. But why don't you tell him the truth? Are you really going to let him marry her?"

I waited until a few people in suits walked by. "What else can I do? I can't make him remember, and reminding him of his past when he's not ready could cause a relapse."

She looked at me sympathetically. "I understand all that, but if you don't tell him, who will?"

I thought about Jasmine and Joe. Would they have a chance to try again? I couldn't. I felt like it was breaking a rule, and Cam would be magically transported back into a coma. Just in case that was true, I had to stick to my guns.

"It's Cam's choice in the end."

A thought came to my mind; there was one thing I could do, but I'd have to wait until Millie wasn't watching. I cleared my throat just as my phone buzzed with a text from Millie. "Time to go."

"Well, regardless of what happens with Cam, we'd love to have you here. I'll check on your work in the next few hours, and we can talk when things settle."

I smiled. "Thanks. I really appreciate it."

Maybe things would be okay with me after all. I might not have the love of my life, but at least I had an opportunity for a better job. Maybe, just maybe, this mess actually would have a purpose, because right now, I could see no silver lining.

Although . . .

I froze as a thought crashed into me with the force of a train. *What have I done?* Cam worked at the hospital, the hospital I would be working for if I took this job. I would see him all the time.

That would be the worst possible thing for my resolve to stay away from him.

221

I sighed and made my way back to the chapel. I couldn't help but be disappointed that Plan B already seemed like a failure.

Chapter 26

I wish I could say the rest of the afternoon went horribly, and that Cam finally noticed how uptight his fiancée was, but when he returned to the rehearsal and heard the details of the wedding, he was intent on listening to me fill him in on every detail. Millie stood smugly nearby, so I couldn't get a word in edgewise about any other topic.

Somehow, I pulled the whole wedding together, and things were set for the next day. I doubted most of the guests Millie finally decided on would come last minute, but I made plenty of calls. I stayed as long as I could to see if Millie would leave, but it seemed like she was camping out just in case I tried anything.

After work, I sat in my car, debating whether I should wait a few hours and then try to talk to him, or if I should just leave fate alone. I was sure Millie was watching his phone very carefully, so that wasn't an option.

In the end, I decided to do half of my plan. I had thought about the journal when I was talking to Cassie, a way I could remind Cam of how he felt about Millie.

And if he happened to keep reading, maybe he'd remember about me too. Hopefully that didn't break any rules of my promise.

Eventually, hunger became too great for me to ignore, and I decided on a burger, fries, and a shake to help me make a decision that might affect the next day. I bought and ate my dinner in the hospital cafeteria and headed to Cam's room with his journal. If Millie caught me, I could say I was returning what was his. But hopefully that wouldn't happen.

I felt like a spy once I reached Cam's floor. I snuck around corners, scurried down the hall, and peeked into his room. He was sleeping and all alone. I hurried inside, then shut and locked the door.

My heart pounded heavily inside my chest, ricocheting and making a mess of my gut. If I didn't get out of here fast, I'd lose my dinner all over the floor. Instead of waking him like I badly wanted to do, I gently laid the journal next to him on the bed and covered it up the best I could with his blanket. It was inches away from his fingertips, so hopefully, he would find it before Millie did.

The movement had jarred him a bit, and his eyes moved rapidly behind his closed lids. I wanted so badly to lean over and touch him, but those days of wishing and wanting were over. All I wanted now was for him to know the truth about how he felt about Millie.

"Goodbye, Cam," I whispered aloud. "Take care of yourself for me." His face showed no sign of recognition, so I added, "I'll see you in my dreams."

I called Jasmine on my way out. They were the last guests I needed to call, though Millie had told me to strip them from the list entirely. I just couldn't.

Jasmine answered after the first ring. "Rory, are you okay?"

I smiled. "Yes, I'm fine. I just wanted to invite you . . . to the wedding tomorrow."

Jasmine sighed. "They're still going through with it?"

"Yes. Have you had a chance to see him since the other day?"

"No. We've tried to call, and all of our calls are blocked by Millie. Joe's really down about everything. He's tried texting and calling. He stopped by yesterday, but Millie was there and sent him away. I feel like we're not doing enough for him. He should know who he's marrying."

I sighed. "I know. We can only hope he will pull through this on his own, find his own way out of the mess."

"And if he doesn't?" Jasmine asked, her voice breaking.

"Then you help him pick up the pieces when things start to fall apart."

After giving her the time and place of the wedding I hung up, feeling sick to my stomach. I went home, took a few aspirin, and called it a night. I should have been tired, but I lay awake, allowing myself to replay for the last time every moment I had shared with Cam.

I was sure I knew what it felt like to be broken

inside, where I couldn't breathe. Couldn't think. But it hadn't even scratched the surface of how I felt. Tomorrow, it would be all over, and maybe then I could finally move on.

The next morning was a nightmare. Literally. I had to peel myself out of bed and force myself to wear something nice to a wedding I vehemently did not want to go to. Luckily, I didn't have to help the bride with any preparations. Her mom and friends had come to support her.

When I showed up to the hospital, many hours before the ceremony, her mom was drinking something from a flask in her purse.

"Hey, Help," Millie called to me. She had taken to calling me that since finding out about Cam and I. "Fix this flower arrangement. It looks off-center."

The flower arrangement looked perfect. I rolled my eyes and fiddled with it until she turned her attention to something else. *Good thing I emailed my resignation this morning.* She'd probably be too busy to read it until after her honeymoon, and by the time she returned, I would only have a few days left.

The day dragged on, and when Millie left the room to get ready, I sighed with relief. I needed time away so I wouldn't have to hear her talk about "Phillip" anymore. Was I really doing the right thing by not coming out and telling him the truth? I didn't have to tell him about our past, but I couldn't just let him walk blindly into a relationship with someone who would use him.

I needed to do more. He deserved to know. After Millie left, and an hour before the reception started, I made a run for Cam's room.

One of Millie's friends was standing at the door when I passed. I tried to keep walking, hoping she hadn't seen my intention to stop, but she reached out and grabbed my shoulder hard. "Hey, Millie warned me about you."

I snatched my arm away and took a step back. "I'm the event planner. I have to make sure everyone is ready."

She was a redhead with too many freckles. She shook her head and closed the door so I wouldn't be able to see in. "You're supposed to stay away from this room. Hands off."

A bitter taste entered my mouth, and I felt like giving Millie's friend the identical eye treatment I'd given Millie last week. Sure Millie's eye was covered up well with makeup, but I knew and she knew, and there was a perverse satisfaction in that. This girl would swell up and Millie could see that I was done being nice to her and all her people. Instead, I kept my hands tightly at my side. "I was just checking to make sure he has everything he needs."

She smirked at me. "Believe me. He does."

Gritting my teeth and keeping in all the obscenities I wanted to say, I spun on my heel. The sting of regret settled in hard as I walked further away from Cam. I had ruined my chance last night. Why hadn't I told him when he was alone?

I made it to the nearest bathroom before I lost my composure, and it took me several minutes before I felt confident enough to leave. I retouched my makeup from the supplies in my purse and dragged myself out to finish overseeing the wedding.

A half hour before the reception, guests started arriving. Most of them were friends or family of Millie, but a few friends of Cam's were present, including Joe and Jasmine.

Jasmine cornered me as soon as she saw me. "Girl, do you know Millie won't let us get a word in, won't let him answer the phone. She won't let him breathe enough to remember he doesn't love her. Millie's had her dad stand guard around him."

I held a finger to my mouth and glanced around to see who'd heard. Thank goodness Millie was in another room. "Cam's made his choice," I said, seating them.

"That's because he doesn't realize there's another option. Rory, he loves you," Joe said, refusing to sit down.

I smiled, a real smile even. "I appreciate you saying that. But this is happening, and there's no way you or I would ruin Cam's wedding day with a 'what if' scenario. Maybe he's changed. Maybe he's remembered why he loves her. And if not, he'll need you two to help him move on. I can't be that person anymore."

Joe grumbled something but settled against the pew, and I returned to seating the guests. There were a handful more of Cam's friends, and even though I tried not to pay attention, they looked just as unsettled to be at this wedding as Joe.

Finally, Cam came into the room, dressed in a tuxedo, and carrying an IV bag and cart with him. The tux fit him perfectly, and a painful jolt went through me as I looked at him like that for the last time. After this moment, he would be a married man.

He waved politely at a few guests, including Joe and Jasmine. He smiled at me when I caught his eye, but just as quickly moved on to focusing on other guests. I groaned inwardly.

The journal, my last hope, hadn't worked. Either he had read it and he didn't feel the same, or the journal was taken from him and he had no clue about it. Either way, I had to accept that this, whatever we had been, was definitely over.

I took my seat at the back of the room, making sure everything I was in charge of was in order. Too soon, the Wedding March started, and we all turned to the doorway to see Millie dressed in the most expensive wedding dress I'd ever seen. Way too fancy for a hospital, though of course, she looked beautiful. She had hired someone to do her makeup, and for once, I could see her eyes without the spidery mess around her lashes.

Her black hair had been tied back and curled into tight ringlets. Her makeup actually enhanced her face, and even her shoes sparkled. She was the envy of every other girl in that room, especially me.

The preacher started the ceremony, and because Millie had planned for the ceremony to last a total of exactly ten minutes and thirty seconds, the "I do" section came up way too quickly.

Millie confidently said, "I do," with a smile on her face, so wide that I knew her cheeks burned with the effort.

When the preacher gave the same vows to Cam, my heart stilled as I listened to his every word. Cam didn't make it past the first line before he turned to the preacher and then back to Millie.

I stilled, surprised. What was he doing?

"Millie, I-I'm so sorry," Cam said. "I don't love you." He sighed and took her hands in his. "For many months before the accident, I felt us slipping away. The last thing I want to do is hurt you. So, I'm so sorry, but I can't marry you."

Millie's face started to crumple, and she pressed into Cam, filling the space between them. "But, we're supposed to be together. Always."

He shook his head. "I just can't live a lie."

She sobbed.

My heart filled with hope. Had he read the journal? Did he know how I felt? I looked back and forth between the two of them. My hands shook as I silently pled for him to turn to me next.

"And you wait until our wedding to tell me?!"

He sighed. "You didn't really give me a choice. I've been awake for less than a week and you jumped on this opportunity to take me blindly. You even made me resign a marriage license the day after I woke up. Who does that?"

"I . . . We love each other. It just makes sense for us to be together."

He shook his head sadly. "You might feel that way, but I know now that I haven't felt that way in a long time."

Millie's face fell, all hopes of getting married dashed before her eyes. Again, I felt sad that this was happening to her. I would feel bad for any bride being dumped at the altar.

But I couldn't be too sad while my soul cheered

for joy. They were not getting married!

The crowd erupted in whispers, and Millie's mascara trails made it obvious how she was feeling. She turned and glared in my direction.

I slid down in my seat, worried she would see the guilt in my eyes.

"Fine," she screeched. "It wouldn't have worked anyway." She ran out of the room, cursing and screaming all the way down the hall until an elevator muffled her tirade.

Her friends and family followed closely behind, grumbling their complaints of 'wasting our time' and 'so inappropriate of him'."

Cam's side of the room remained seated. When it was quiet again, he sighed and turned to the few left in the audience.

"I'm sorry you came out today, but I have a small feeling that our relationship wouldn't have worked out."

The room erupted with laughs and a couple of cheers, and, as Cam headed down the aisle to leave, his friends got up and followed him. I watched as he made it to the back where I sat, but instead of making a connection, his eyes went right through me.

My shoulders fell, and I slumped back against the hard bench. He didn't remember. I tried not to feel devastated; after all, I had possibly just saved him from a terrible marriage. Cam was an amazing person with a big heart . . . even if he couldn't remember that his heart had once been mine.

Chapter 27

It was easier than I thought to return to work for the remaining ten days. Even though Millie didn't get married, it was rumored she still took the planned honeymoon to South America, accompanied by an old flame.

I went to the gym every day, not to see Cam, but to run. Mindful of my promise and not wanting to jeopardize his recovery, I stayed away completely. Running a 5K would be a breeze when spring came.

When I went back to talk to the hospital event coordinator, I was hired on the spot. She seemed more than happy for me to start whenever I wanted.

I spent nights at the ninnies', ignoring my pain and getting lost in their constant chatter. But I never really forgot about Cam. I was just managing. Not really moving on.

On the second to last day of my old job, an interim

General Manager showed up, claiming to be taking over for Millie until new management was chosen. Even if it wasn't Millie running the resort, I didn't want to be on a property that was owned by her father. The new manager seemed nice, and when I explained my sudden departure the next day with a recommendation for Brittney to take over as Events Coordinator, he was happy to oblige.

I spent the last day prepping Brittney and making sure she had plenty to keep her busy for a long time. Even though Millie was gone, I wasn't sure I could return to the resort business. It held too many sad memories of multiple kinds. The hospital would keep me busy until I could find something else.

After my last night of work, I met with Cassie and arranged the details of my new job. The hospital wasn't able to match my salary completely, but the medical benefits well exceeded the loss in monthly pay. On my way out, Cassie grabbed my arm.

"Hey, have you heard from Cam? Seen him at all since his . . . wedding?"

I shook my head. "I haven't. I guess I should just be happy it didn't happen."

Cassie gave me a sympathetic smile. "Well, you should know, he left the hospital yesterday with a full recovery. I can't believe he came back to work today."

I smiled, though my heart leaped inside me with this news. "Sounds like him."

She shook her head. "He looks like the stuffing's been kicked out of him."

"He's been through a lot. I am sure it will take a while for him to look like himself again."

More than anything, Cam needed time to

remember who he was, and I needed time to adjust to normalcy again and to heal.

I took the weekend off and spent some time shopping at my favorite thrift store. I found a cute sundress for next season and pair of bangled bracelets. On my way to the cash register, I saw a jean jacket that would be perfect for a casual date, then dropped it on the floor.

Memories of Cam flooded my mind. I had been trying so long to keep him out of my thoughts that I didn't realize he was a part of my heart and soul now.

I didn't know how to get over this feeling, but maybe some time to allow myself to think about him, to give myself permission to relive every second together, would help give me a little closure. I could have driven to the gym or the ski hill or some other place we had gone together, but it would have been too much. I remembered about Cam's lookout spot that overlooked the entire city. We had never had a chance to go together, and it felt right that I went without him. Once I started thinking about it, I couldn't drive the car fast enough.

The pull-off at the top of the canyon was abandoned and breathtaking. The city lights twinkled below like tiny lightning bugs having a reunion. With the added light of the moon, I could see perfectly, and I made my way to the back of the Jeep to open the hatch and find the spare blanket I kept there. I took my time spreading it out in the back of the vehicle, drinking in the landscape around me.

A branch crackled behind me, and I spun around to see Cam standing behind me. My breath caught in my throat as our eyes connected. He was here. Right now. Was I dreaming? Was he a ghost? Had he been hurt again?

"You're here," he said a little surprised.

"I'm here," I said back. I looked out at the city and then back at him. "Want to sit?"

"Yeah. I've wanted to come up here for a while, to think, but I was only released the other day."

I nodded. "I heard. I'm glad you're doing well. You gave us a scare there."

He chuckled and took a seat next to me. "I guess so."

There wasn't a ton of room in the vehicle because of my emergency kit and case of water, so we were close enough that our legs touched.

"How are you?" I asked.

"Not bad actually. I'm back at work, and it feels good to be active again. How about you? I heard from a little birdie that you left the resort."

My smile disappeared. "Yeah, I didn't realize that giving up something I wanted so badly could actually make me happier. Millie treats her employees worse than she treated you, if you can imagine that."

He frowned, and I realized too late my mistake.

"Um, sorry," I started. "That was really insensitive. I shouldn't be—"

He held up a hand to stop me. "You don't have to explain. I know Millie well enough to know she was taking advantage of you and me. And I wouldn't give up your resort dream so soon. I have something in the works that I might need help with."

I lifted an eyebrow. "Are you why the resort just changed hands? An interim manager introduced himself a day before I left."

He nodded. "It will take a while to get things organized, but don't shut that door too soon."

I nodded and tried to hide my smile. "I'll try to keep it open for a while."

He returned my smile, and we looked out at the scenery again, both content to sit in silence. My nerves buzzed now that he was so close and alive next to me. Finally, I broke the silence.

"So, how's Swordy doing?" I slapped a hand to my mouth. Of course I shouldn't know who Swordy is. What was I trying to do here? Couldn't I keep it together for even a few minutes?

"You know about my fish?"

I took a deep breath. There was no way I'd tell him everything. I didn't want him running from the car. But maybe I could tell him a few things, just to see how he'd react.

"Yes, I know Swordy." His eyes showed interest instead of caution, so I continued. "Like how you have a room full of Avenger memorabilia."

He laughed. "Well everyone knows that. Joe could have told you that."

"Well, he didn't."

He lifted his eyebrows, but humored me with a smile. "What else do you know about me?"

I smiled. "That your favorite place to go and think is right here. You texted me about it before our first date."

He held his chin in a thoughtful gesture. "Anything else."

"That you have a house key in a plant by the front door," I said, smiling a bit more.

A look of surprise crossed his face. "But how

would you know—"

"And that you keep your journal under a hidden door in your closet."

His hand dropped from his chin, and his mouth fell open. "Okay, who have you talked to? Did Millie tell you that?"

I smiled uneasily. "No. Remember, she didn't know where it was?"

He opened his mouth but then closed it. "She didn't. But I thought she had found it. She brought it to my bedside the night before we were married."

My heart skipped a beat. He had seen the journal. "That's right. You did have your journal, but Millie didn't bring it to you."

"But then how do you know about it?"

I sighed. "Before your coma, you and I were . . . dating."

A small smile crept back to his face. "Joe tried to explain some of this to me the other day, but I thought he was off his rocker. How could I forget dating someone? Why didn't I remember you when I woke up?"

I shrugged. "I've thought those same thoughts for the last ten days."

"We only saw each other a few times before you—" My throat tightened, and I couldn't say any more. I had been so close to losing him. Putting my emotions to the side, I thought about his journal entries and that he'd admitted there how he felt about me. "You really liked that girl you spoke about in your last few entries, but it was so early, and we had shared so little together. I'm not surprised you don't remember."

He looked out at the evening sky, a pensive look replacing his confusion. "It took me a while to believe what I'd written. I couldn't, can't remember anything from that time."

I frowned, a little disappointed that the memories we'd made before and during his coma hadn't returned, but I wasn't going to bring it up. "Well, it's okay. I'm just glad you're not with Millie anymore. Why *did* you decide to break things off?"

He cleared his throat. "Well, that's a strange story for me. If it was you who gave me back my journal, it makes sense what was going on, but at the time, the entries you wrote in my journal sounded like someone who knew me well and who loved me in return. So I thought maybe Millie had written everything. But when I asked her, she had no idea what I was talking about. I knew then it wasn't her."

I nodded. "Surprise! It was me."

"But how could you— How did you know how you felt after only a few dates with me?"

I shifted away from him. Now came the crazy ghost part I would keep to myself. "I don't know. I guess I just had a good feeling about us."

He turned to me, confusion on his face. "Why didn't you say anything? When I woke up, why didn't you tell me all this?"

I looked out at the night. It couldn't hurt to tell him this part of the story. No ghosts involved. "Uh, well, that is the superstitious part of this story. I promise I'm not crazy or that I believe in crazy, paranormal stories, but when you didn't wake up right away, I made a promise."

"A promise?" he said, more to himself than to me.

I nodded. "When you didn't stir a bit after they removed the breathing tube, I promised myself that if you woke up, I would go away and let Millie have you. I would give you up completely."

Cam turned back to studying the city. The silence pressed upon me so much I felt my heart thumping in my ears.

Say something.

Finally, he spoke, more quietly than before. "You would sacrifice what we had so I could live?"

My throat tightened. "Yes, Cam." There was no hesitation in my voice now. I knew how *I* felt about him. "So that's why I stayed away. I thought I would mess up something, and you'd go back into a coma. Anyway, our time together taught me a lot . . . about life in general, and I don't regret it."

He was quiet again for so long I was worried he was upset. At last, he said, "So am I a good kisser?"

I burst out laughing. *That came from out of nowhere.* "What?"

"Am I a good kisser?" he asked again, emphasizing every word.

I smiled and looked away, out again at the twinkling lights of the city. "Well, technically, before your accident, you only kissed me on the cheek."

"Hmm..." he hummed. "So you liked me, and I didn't even have to prove I'm an excellent kisser."

I laughed. "I guess so, though I guess I did cheat once."

He lifted an eyebrow. "Cheated, huh?"

I sighed. "Another superstitious part of me. You sure are learning a lot of my quirks tonight."

"I like quirks," he said with an air of confidence.

239

"So how did you cheat this one time?"

I smiled, remembering. "When the doctors came in to release you from care, I made them stop right before they cut off your oxygen. As carefully as I could, I kissed you goodbye, you know, just in case you didn't come out of it. The three people I'm closest to, I call them the ninnies, they're superstitious, even more so than I am. They think that my kiss woke you up."

A soft smile played at the edges of his mouth. He lifted his hand to my face and tucked some of my hair behind my ear. Then gently, he took my hand in his. "I wish I remembered all of this. I don't know you, but I want to. Are you willing to give us another run?"

I smiled and nodded, giddy at the thought of rediscovering our connection. He came closer to me, and I didn't hesitate. His lips were soft against mine, and, as he deepened the kiss, I inhaled his scent of leather, cologne, and almonds. His kiss was more than I could've ever imagined. Soft and passionate all at the same time. I melted against him, memorizing every inch of his face with my hands.

He backed away after a few seconds. "How did I do?"

I laughed and stroked the side of his cheek. "You could use some practice."

He widened his eyes and moved in for another kiss.

After a few more moments that seemed to take not just mine but also his breath away, I sighed. "I better go. I start my new job at the hospital tomorrow."

"You're going to work at the hospital?"

I nodded, worried that would mean I wouldn't be able to date him now. "Is that an issue, if we're dating? I don't know if we are, but if we were and I worked there, would it be a—"

Cam lifted his finger to my mouth to shush me. Then he kissed me once more. A soft, quick brush of his lips. "It won't be a problem. But if you need any assurance, I should probably do this right. Rory, will you be my girlfriend?"

I laughed and brought his face closer to mine so that our noses touched. "As long as you want me."

Epilogue

It's amazing how quickly things happened after that. Cam and I started dating steady for the second time, and I fell in love all over again.

My hospital job ended a few weeks after it started. Cam came to me with a business proposition. Millie had sold him all her shares to the resort. He asked me to manage the resort for him, and I jumped at the opportunity. It felt so great to return to my old stomping grounds. Of course, I asked Brittney to remain the Event Coordinator and I contacted a lot of the previous staff and offered them their jobs back.

Things were finally returning to normal. To a better normal than I'd ever had. Though his memories never returned, I tried to relive each memory we'd shared to jog his memory.

After our first month of dating, I introduced him to Snowball and the ninnies. They approved, especially Snowball. He even stole Cam's keys to show him how much.

Six months into dating, I felt like the luckiest girl in the world. I bounced around my kitchen, beaming happily and frequently glancing out the window. Cam was on his way over. I was making him a real Italian dinner of spaghetti and meatballs, and we had plans to see each other almost every night this week.

So when he walked in with a frown on his face, my light, happy feeling turned to fear. "What's wrong? Did Millie try to contact you again?" My thoughts jumped around to a dozen possible negative scenarios.

In the middle of my awful thoughts, Cam began to smile. "I have something for you. But you have to close your eyes."

"Okay," I said, obediently closing my eyes.

"Hold out your hand," he told me, and I did. He laid something smooth and square in my hands, almost like a deck of cards.

"Can I open them?" I asked.

"Yep," he said, his voice a little higher than normal.

True to my guess, a deck of cards sat in my hands. "Go Fish cards?" I said, reading the top of the box. "Do you like this game?" I asked, "because you know I can stomp anyone."

Cam looked at me meaningfully. "I know you can."

I stared down at the box. How did he know that? The only time we had played cards together had been…

I snapped my head up at the same time Cam's face brightened into a smile.

243

"You remember?" I asked, my voice breaking a little.

Cam nodded. "Every tiny little thing. It's been coming back to me in pieces for a while now, and every time I relived a dream or a memory that came to me, I wrote it down in my journal." He pulled his journal out of his bag and flipped through it. The book was nearly full of writing.

I pulled him in close for a hug. "That's great, Cam."

"I can't believe you didn't tell me about how I appeared to you in the form of a ghost."

I shrugged and laughed. "Would you have believed me?"

He chuckled. "Probably not. Well, open the cards, and we'll play while dinner's cooking."

I obliged, cutting the tape seal on the card deck. I pulled out one card and gasped. I pulled out more cards, tears slipping down my cheeks now. Each card had a memory we had shared together, some during our first try at dating, most from our more recent relationship. Pictures of us were taped to some of them, and others were just his words.

"Oh my gosh, I love them. Can I read them all right now?"

He chuckled. "I was really hoping you'd say that. Take your time. I forgot something in the car."

I sat down and looked at every card. So that's why he had taken it upon himself to take so many pictures in the last months. It had driven me crazy, but he was so cute that I couldn't turn him down when he pulled out his camera.

Now I had every single one to cherish and

remember. It took about five minutes to make it to the bottom of the stack. Finally, I picked up the last card. There was a picture of us standing on his deck together outside his room. When we'd stood on his deck for the first time, I knew I loved him and there was no going back.

He had taken a picture with his phone, and texted it to me, and for months it had been my favorite thing to look at. I flipped it over to read the story but the card only had a few words.

"As long as you want me."

I looked up from the cards, a sly smile on my face. It had become our routine answer that we said when responding to each other.

Cam still wasn't back. He deserved some major points for this project. I stood up and searched for him outside through the living room window, but his truck was empty. I turned around and there he was.

On one knee.

I covered my mouth with one hand. "Are you—"

"Shhh," he said, making me laugh. "You're making me nervous." He held out both hands, and I came as close as I could without knocking him over.

"In the past six months, I have fallen in love with this strong, beautiful person, who was not only patient and kind, but was willing to sacrifice our relationship to save my life. There is no one else in this world that makes me as happy as you do."

My throat tightened, and I blinked away happy tears. I squeezed his hand, and he squeezed mine in return.

"Now that I have all of my memories of you back, I have not fallen for you once, but twice. If we

245

continue like we have been, I will keep on falling. I am so in love with you, Rory Lee. Will you be my wife and make me the happiest man in the world?"

I smiled and kissed him softly. "As long as you want me."

PLEASE LEAVE A REVIEW

If you enjoyed reading *Man of My Dreams*, please leave a quick review at your online book retailer. Like slipping a generous tip to your waiter, reviews let authors know that you appreciate all of our hard work. Most of the time, we have no idea whether our readers have liked or even finished our stories. Writing is mentally and emotionally grueling, and a few kind words about the story go a long way and keep us going. Thank you for sharing the journey.

Can't get enough?
Try Diving for Love.
It's the perfect mix of young love with a touch of suspense.

ABOUT THE AUTHOR

After going on over 150 first dates, Jenny has a wealth of dating experience. She lives with her husband and three kids near the mountains, drawing inspiration from the constant ups and downs of relationships. When she's not writing clean, swoony romances, she's following some other dream to make a difference in the world.